'Anybody wou
like me.'

Abbie glared at ..... Anybody would be right,' she muttered.

Without warning, Leo swung the car off the road and screeched to a halt in a lay-by.

'Abbie, Abbie. You like me—even though you might not want to. And you want me—even though you think it's a lousy idea. I do, too, but——' His shrug was Gallic and very expressive.

She blushed. 'Dream on,' she muttered.

Dear Reader

August is for holidays and the four books this month should beguile your time. Caroline Anderson offers ROLE PLAY, where GP Leo hides his emotions; family difficulties abound in Lilian Darcy's CONFLICTING LOYALTIES alongside an insight to a burns unit; ONGOING CARE by Mary Hawkins continues the theme raised in PRIORITY CARE and updates those people; and, in A DEDICATED VET by Carol Wood, Gina has a lot to prove about herself. All good stuff!

The Editor

!!!STOP PRESS!!! If you enjoy reading these medical books, have you ever thought of writing one? We are always looking for new writers for LOVE ON CALL, and want to hear from you. Send for the guidelines, with SAE, and start writing!

Caroline Anderson's nursing career was brought to an abrupt halt by a back injury, but her interest in medical things led her to work first as a medical secretary, and then, after completing her teacher training, as a lecturer in medical office practice to trainee medical secretaries. In addition to writing, she also runs her own business from her home in rural Suffolk, where she lives with her husband, two daughters, mother and dog.

Recent titles by the same author:

A MAN OF HONOUR
PICKING UP THE PIECES
SECOND THOUGHTS

ROLE PLAY

BY
CAROLINE ANDERSON

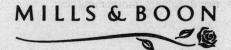

MILLS & BOON

MILLS & BOON LIMITED
ETON HOUSE, 18–24 PARADISE ROAD
RICHMOND, SURREY, TW9 1SR

First published in Great Britain 1994 by Mills & Boon Limited

© Caroline Anderson 1994

Australian copyright 1994   Philippine copyright 1994 This edition 1994

ISBN 0 263 78731 1

Set in 10 on 12 pt Linotron Times 03-9408-49764

Typeset in Great Britain by Centracet, Cambridge Made and printed in Great Britain

CHAPTER ONE

ABIGAIL PEARCE was going to marry a doctor. It wasn't a conscious decision, rather something she had always known and accepted.

What she also knew, after a week in general practice, was that there was no way he would be a GP!

The lifestyle was horrendous. Paper mountains, patients with nothing wrong with them and patients who were clearly dying and had left it too late to do anything, all muddled up with legions of bronchitics and asthmatics — and the whole lot of them tied together with endless miles of tangled red tape!

It didn't suit Abbie's chaotic and ephemeral mind at all, and as she drove towards the surgery on that lovely August morning she felt the now familiar panic tightening her chest. What would she do if someone came in and she wasn't sure about her diagnosis? For the first time in her life there wasn't someone else to ask, a registrar to fall back on at a moment's notice.

Not that she was really alone. There were other doctors in the practice, she was hardly single-handed, but the senior partner Dr Williams was off sick with a bad back, Dr Patel didn't seem inclined to be over-friendly towards her, and Dr Chandler was on holiday. Only Peter Sargent had been welcoming, and Abbie was fairly sure it was because all his 'heartsink' patients had transferred themselves to her within the first thirty seconds, or so it seemed.

And her heart was sinking, too, at the thought of the rest of the year yawning away ahead of her like something out of a horror movie. It wasn't going to be improved by the fact that she was late, either.

Her inventive mind busily working on excuses, she swung into the car park and skidded to an undignified halt. There was a red sports car — well, it had been once, about thirty years ago, she thought disparagingly — abandoned across the entrance, the roof down and Tina Turner blaring forth from the open cockpit. She had nearly hit it — not that she would have done it a great deal of harm, when all was said and done, but her own could have sustained considerable damage——

A car tooted furiously behind her, and she inched forwards until she was nearly touching the muddy bumper. What a heap!

And blocking her space. She climbed out and locked her car, checking to see how far out into the road it was hanging. Not very. She might just get away with it until whoever owned it moved the horrible relic.

She squeezed past the front of the car, smearing mud on her jacket as she went, and ran up the steps into the office at the back of the surgery where the practice meeting was drawing to a close.

'Sorry I'm late,' she apologised, scattering her smile among the assembled company. 'Some yob's abandoned a heap of scrap in the car park and I couldn't get in.'

'Ah.'

Her eyes swivelled to the owner of the voice, and as their gazes locked a tiny quiver of something unfamiliar curled around her throat and tightened.

She watched, mesmerised, as the stranger unravelled his long legs and stood up, the soft battered leather of his jacket tugging over his broad shoulders as he pushed the chair in, sending her pulse rocketing; confused, she dropped her eyes and they lingered over lean hips and long, long legs in faded denim jeans that hugged his body intimately, finally crumpling to a halt at the ancient trainers on his feet.

She relaxed with a tiny sigh of relief. He looked for all the world like an overgrown college student — or one of her brothers, she thought absently, and then found herself trapped again by those extraordinary blue-gold eyes.

He was laughing at her, aware of her minute inspection of his person and supremely, masculinely confident that he would have passed muster. As he returned the compliment with a quick, appreciative once-over, all her muscles leapt to attention again, and she felt the heat rising from her toes upwards until she flushed almost guiltily.

'I'll move it.'

His voice was rich and deep and gravelly, and completed the process of cerebral disintegration that had started the second she clapped eyes on him. 'What?' she said absently.

'The car.'

She gathered her scattered thought-processes rapidly. 'Oh. It's yours, then,' she managed inanely, and to her disgust and humiliation her voice sounded breathless and far-away.

His smile was brilliant, teasing, wicked. '"Heap of scrap",' he said softly. 'Is that any way to speak of my charger, when I've come dashing back from my holiday like a knight in shining armour to rescue you from the clutches of my colleagues? Not to mention calling me a yob!'

'Oh, God,' she mumbled under her breath, and felt the heat rising in her cheeks. Had she really said all that?

He shrugged away from the table and held out his hand. 'You must be Abigail Pearce. Leo Chandler — yob, doctor, knight in shining armour — at your service, ma'am.' His hand was warm and dry and firm, engulfing hers and making her feel unexpectedly feminine and fragile. She was stunned at the shock-wave that rippled up her arm from the brief contact, and as soon as she could she whipped her hand away and tucked it into her pocket.

He smiled knowingly. 'I'll move the "heap of scrap".'

And with a grin he sauntered out through the door and left her standing rooted to the spot, her mouth hanging slightly open.

A slight noise behind her brought her back to reality with a bump, and, snapping her mouth shut, she turned back to the others.

'Oh, God,' she repeated, and slumped against the wall.

Peter Sargent chuckled. 'That'll get you off to a flying start — good job he doesn't take offence easily.'

Abbie was still feeling thoroughly rattled by the encounter, and she was sure it showed. To escape from Ravi Patel's knowing black eyes, she went back outside to move her car just as Leo Chandler loped up the steps.

'There you are,' he said with that spectacular grin. 'Plenty of room now, even for you. Oh, by the way,

Dr Pearce, we need to have a chat some time. Colin's asked me to take over your training until he's back, so we could do with sorting out a few things. Coffee suit you?'

'That'll be fine,' she mumbled, stunned again by the amazing eyes. Or was it the man behind them?

She climbed into her car, over-conscious of his lazy scrutiny, and crashed the gears. What on earth had got into her? She was twenty-seven, for goodness' sake — she'd survived all her brothers' friends, and the endless stream of available men at medical school — why this particular man, and why now of all times? He was a shocking flirt, too, a superficial, womanising tease, not at all the sort of man she had in mind.

So why the damage to her pulse-rate?

Must be a virus, she thought with the last vestige of humour, and, crunching the gears again, she eased into the tiny space he had left her and struggled out.

'Poor little car,' he murmured as she reached the top of the steps.

'You put me off,' she said crossly, and then was angry with herself for giving it away.

His grin broadened. 'Interesting.'

'I'm glad you think so,' she replied as coolly as she could manage, and, sucking in her breath, she squeezed past him through the gap.

Or she would have done if he hadn't moved his arm up to block her path.

She came to a dead halt, her breasts pressed against his well-muscled forearm, her heart doing a tango against her ribs.

'Don't forget our date.'

She stepped back and looked up into his eyes,

bewildered by his words and by the flood of sensation that was swamping her. 'Date?' she said weakly.

'Coffee — to talk about your training programme.'

'Oh — yes, of course.'

'You're blushing,' he said with evident amusement, and she felt the colour deepen.

'Rubbish, it's hot. Excuse me, I have a surgery. . .'

'Ah, yes.' He moved out of her way, almost reluctantly, and she felt his eyes on her until she reached the door at the far side of the office.

And not only *his* eyes. Ravi, too, was watching her, her sloe eyes intent, accusing.

So that's the way of it, Abbie thought. Well, I'm no threat to you, Ravi, dear. Have him, and welcome.

She shut her surgery door behind her with relief.

It was short-lived. The second her last patient exited the surgery, Leo Chandler was in, two cups of coffee balanced in one hand, a file in the other.

'What kept you?' she asked drily.

He grinned his appreciation. 'Me?' he murmured innocently. 'I've been dangling around for ages while you built relationships with your patients. "Good morning, that looks nasty, have a bottle of pills, goodbye." '

She sighed and leant back in the chair, lifting the heavy mass of red-gold hair that tumbled in cheerful profusion over her shoulders. Her neck was hot — really she should have worn it up, or at least tied back, but she had been on the drag——

'Why *were* you late, by the way?' he asked as if he read her mind. 'I mean, pulling up behind my "heap of scrap" must have taken you — oh, thirty seconds? At the outside.'

She sighed again. Clearly that remark was going to haunt her forever more. 'Time isn't my absolutely best thing,' she confessed with a rueful grin.

'You don't say.' He handed her the coffee and sprawled in the chair beside her desk, long legs stuck out in front, his cup balanced precariously on his belt-buckle. He had changed into a pair of cool cotton trousers and a soft, stonewashed shirt, the cuffs turned back to reveal the scatter of fine golden hair that dusted his wrists and forearms. The trousers were much less conspicuously masculine than the jeans had been, and yet — She looked away, her cheeks heating again.

Her embarrassment wasn't eased by his evident enjoyment of it.

'So,' he said suddenly. 'Your training. Done any role-play exercises before?'

She groaned and rolled her eyes. 'Role play?'

'Mmm. Doctor, doctor, I think I'm a pair of curtains. Pull yourself together, man. That sort of thing.'

She giggled despite herself. 'Not for years. Why?'

He shrugged. 'Because it can be very useful for exploring the unsolved mysteries of doctor-patient relationships.'

He shifted in his chair, and swung his eyes away from her, suddenly awkward.

'Before we get on to that, there's something I wanted to ask you about — something personal.'

Her heart tightened in anticipation. Not that date he had teased her with, surely? But what else. . .?

'Ask away,' she prompted.

He was silent for a second, then he spoke in a rush,

his voice strained. 'I'm having problems — personal problems. Well, sexual problems, I suppose. I'm — I think I'm impotent.'

She laughed. She didn't mean to, but the idea of the man in front of her having any kind of sexual problem at all was just absurd in the extreme.

He met her eyes, his own reproving. 'Tut-tut. You aren't supposed to laugh, you're supposed to ask me when it started, how many times it's happened, if it's always the same pattern, if it's only when I'm with a partner or — '

'All right, all right!' She threw her hands up in the air in an attitude of surrender, and tried to school her expression. 'You just caught me unprepared.'

'And would you be prepared if someone came up to you and said something like that in a supermarket, or in a restaurant?'

'Don't be ridiculous! They wouldn't — '

'Oh no?' He leant back and shook his head. 'Don't be too sure. I was in the bar at the squash club last winter and someone came up to me — total stranger — and asked me what he should do about his genital warts. I told him to see his GP, and he said I was his GP, and what should he do?'

'What did you tell him?'

'Come and see me at the surgery. What else? If you give advice when you can't make an examination, then you could be in deep legal trouble. Once you've started to give any advice at all, you've assumed responsibility for the treatment and the repercussions could be phenomenal. Now, about my sexual problems — '

She laughed again.

He gave her a reproachful look. 'I'm disappointed in

you, Dr Pearce. I thought you might have some new perspective on it that might help me.'

'You're ridiculous,' she told him bluntly, trying hard not to blush. 'The only sexual problem you've got is finding time for all those opportunities in your hectic schedule, I have no doubt.'

He grinned. 'I'm flattered.'

'It wasn't meant to be a compliment,' she said severely, squashing the urge to laugh.

The grin widened. 'Listen, little lady, with my problem I'll take what I can get.'

'Yes, well, just make sure it isn't something nasty.'

'Like Ravinda Patel?'

Her head flew up and their eyes clashed in the sudden silence. 'I thought. . .'

He shook his head slowly. 'Ravi's interested in me, but that's as far as it goes. I've never given her the slightest encouragement.'

'That's not how it looks.'

He shrugged. 'Ravi's got expressive eyes. You'll have to trust me.'

Abbie wasn't sure she dared. Instead, she changed tack. 'Why are you telling me all this?'

'Because the internal politics of any closely knit working community are very sensitive—I just wanted you to know the truth.'

'How do I know it's the truth? How do I know you aren't the world's most monumental flirt who's seen a new toy to play with?'

'Me?' His expression of injured innocence had to be seen to be believed. Only the wicked twinkling of his extraordinary blue-gold eyes gave him away.

'You, Leo Chandler,' she said firmly, and quelled

the urge to laugh. 'Anyway, all that besides, what good is role play going to do? We just end up making fools of ourselves and learning nothing we couldn't learn by any other more conventional means.'

'Does that worry you? Making a fool of yourself?'

She shifted awkwardly. How did he know that? 'I like to be in control of a situation,' she compromised.

He laughed. 'In general practice? No way. You want pathology if you want control. Dead people don't do anything unexpected. Live people, now. . .' He shot her a sideways look. 'I have to go out on some calls — come with me. Part of your education.'

'Only if we can go in my car,' she said quickly.

He grinned. 'Mine not good enough for you?' he teased.

She felt herself flush, 'Sorry. I didn't mean that, but it is a little — well — unconventional?' she tried.

He grinned. 'So she is. I'm only using her while my incredibly boring and middle-of-the-road Volvo is being serviced. Topsy usually only comes out on high days and holidays.'

'Topsy?' she said incredulously. Not since her brothers' youth had she heard of a car with a name. 'Why Topsy?'

He shrugged expressively. 'Because of the servicing and repair bills, which, like Topsy, just grow'd and grow'd.'

She laughed softly. 'I'll bet. Look, I'm sorry if I was rude. It's nothing personal, I'm just not into retro-motoring.'

He gave an exaggerated sigh. 'Most women think she's wonderful.'

'Yes, well, I'm not most women,' she told him repressively.

He shot her an odd look. 'No, you're not, are you?' he said, his voice quiet. 'Pity, it could have been fun. Ah, well. . .' He uncoiled his legs and stood up, suddenly almost oppressively large in the small room, and ambled towards the door, whistling softly.

She glared at his departing back, and was treated to the disturbing sight of his neat little bottom and long, lean legs striding casually down the corridor, the soft cotton of his trousers tugging and easing, outlining his firm, muscular thighs with every stride.

He turned at the end and caught her watching him, smiling knowingly at her blush.

'Coming?'

She went—against her better judgement—in Topsy. The car was in distinctly average condition, and she handled, as he put it, 'like a bitch', which did nothing for Abbie's nerves. Nor, frankly, did his proximity in the little car. It was, quite simply, nothing like big enough to keep her as far away from his long, rangy body as she would have liked to be, and every time he changed gear her leg muscles contracted to pull herself further away from him.

Predictably, he noticed. 'Why are you trying to climb out of the door?' he asked casually.

She forced herself to appear relaxed. 'I wasn't—I was just trying to keep out of your way.'

He shot her an evil grin. 'Don't worry on my account,' he told her, and she gave him a dirty look and turned away to stare fixedly out of the side-window, anchoring her hair firmly with one hand to stop it from flying in her eyes.

It was a mercifully short drive, thankfully, through the leafy little Suffolk town of Brocklingford to the house of his first patient.

She was a girl of twelve who suffered from autism, a disorder of behaviour affecting the ability to communicate, where everything said was taken literally — not only words, but tone and movements. Nothing emphatic, nor over-demonstrative, and certainly no physical contact that was a demonstration of affection, Leo told her, because the other and most noticeable feature of autism was an inability to form any relationship or interact normally with another person. It also involved repetitive behaviour patterns, and frustration of those patterns almost inevitably led to major tantrums.

Maxie, she was told, was not severely autistic but had 'autistic features' — meaning, in her case, the lack of social communication skills, and repetitive behaviour coupled with the classic shocking temper. However, she was very gifted musically and also highly intelligent, which was quite unusual.

Abbie was interested, never having had an autistic patient, but she was quite unprepared for the level of literal thinking she was to find.

Maxie's mother greeted them at the door and told them that she had refused to stay in bed. Leo grinned, unsurprised, and followed the woman through to the back of the house.

The girl was pretty in a plain sort of way, but very distant. She was sitting in the dining-room, playing the pino with exquisite sensitivity.

'Hello, Maxie,' Leo said softly.

She stopped playing abruptly and looked at him with

no interest at all. 'Dr Chandler. Why are you here?' she asked tonelessly.

'Your mother said you hadn't been feeling well.'

She turned away, avoiding eye contact. 'Yes. I've got a headache now. Who's that with you?'

'Dr Pearce. She's going to be with the practice for a year. May I have a look at you?'

She turned back again. 'Can't you see me?'

At first Abbie thought she was being cheeky, but then realised she had interpreted Leo's remark quite literally.

'Yes, but I need to look at your eyes and ears and throat with an instrument, and measure your blood-pressure with another, and then perhaps ask you some questions about your diet.'

'I'm not on a diet.'

'The food you eat every day is your diet. We talk about being on a diet when we really mean a reducing diet.'

'Oh.' She turned away again. 'All right.'

'Could you come over here?'

She stood, her movements wooden, and walked over to him. He looked into her eyes with the torch, then checked her ears and took her blood-presssure and temperature.

'You're a bit hot.'

'It's sunny.'

'No, inside. You've got a raised temperature—I think you might have a mild virus that's making you feel ill. May I feel your neck and under your arms?'

She nodded, and he kept his touch to the minimum. Even so, Abbie could see her shrinking.

'Your glands are up—I think you might have glandular fever. Have you had a sore throat recently?'

'You did have one last week,' her mother put in, and Maxie nodded again.

'It was very sore—it still hurts.'

'May I see?'

He shone his torch down her throat and nodded.

'Yes, it looks like a mild case of glandular fever, for which the treatment is rest, rest and more rest. Early nights, not too much activity, and take things easy for a while—maybe even a month. OK?'

Her mother nodded and smiled. 'OK. I had it when I was sixteen, so I can remember what it's like. We'll have to have some early nights, I think.'

Leo smiled, but Maxie turned back to the piano. 'I don't want to rest. Goodbye, Dr Chandler.'

She began to play again, loudly, and her mother shook her head and led them out into the hall, closing the door.

'She really ought to rest, you know,' Leo said seriously.

'I know. I'll do what I can, but she's better off playing the piano than working herself up into a steaming tantrum over it until she collapses with exhaustion.'

'Does she do that?' Abbie asked, amazed that the calm, almost monochromatic child they had just witnessed could throw a tantrum.

Mrs Clarke rolled her eyes. 'Does she ever! You've seen her, haven't you, Dr Chandler?'

'Oh, yes—it's spectacular. She's only calm when she's getting her own way, but she's as stubborn as a mule. Any attempt to coerce her and she flips. Still, you manage her very well.'

The mother shrugged. 'I don't really. We achieve a sort of peace by letting her do things her way. Anything else is cataclysmic! It took some time to learn how to deal with her, and years after that before I could undo the harm I'd done with hugs and cuddles and abortive attempts at discipline.'

Leo nodded. 'The school seems to have helped.'

'Yes — me as much as her. It gives me a break from her but the holidays are just as difficult as ever.'

Leo laid a large, comforting hand on her shoulder and squeezed gently. 'You're doing a grand job — don't lose heart.'

The mother gave them a weary smile. 'Thank you. It helps to hear it.'

As they drove away, Abbie turned to Leo and shook her head. 'How does she cope?'

'How does anyone cope? There but for fortune and all that.'

'Why didn't you take a blood sample to check for mononucleosis?'

He shot her a grin. 'Because Maxie doesn't like needles, and when Maxie doesn't like something she says so — loudly! Anyway, there's no point. Whatever she's got, a few weeks of taking it easy will knock it on the head, and if it doesn't we can deal with it then. Now, we're going to see the rest of my patients, and on the way back to the surgery we're going to pick up some lunch and eat it by the river.'

'Um — do you need me with you?'

He glanced at her, his eyes twinkling wickedly.

'Well, now—there's need, and there's need. What's the problem?'

She gave a tiny snort of disbelief. 'Apart from you? I have things I ought to be doing—I've got an antenatal clinic this afternoon and I wanted to go through the notes, and then there are prescriptions I should be signing and letters to write and——'

'I've done your prescriptions and I'm doing your antenatal clinic this afternoon, so you'll have plenty of time to sit down with Peggy and do the letters. Anything else?'

'Yes,' she said, furiously embarrassed. 'I need the loo.'

He chuckled. 'Trust a woman. Why didn't you go——?'

'Don't! Don't say it! Don't say a word!' she exploded. 'How was I to know you planned a day-long expedition? Anyway, you didn't give me time!'

'It's all that coffee you had for breakfast when you should have been on your way to work,' he teased.

'I didn't have time,' she repeated tightly.

'You amaze me.' He shot her a wink. 'Can you hang on ten minutes? Our next call is in the hospice.'

She subsided huffily. 'I should think so.'

'I hope so—don't want my upholstery ruined.'

She glared at him. 'I think you're a few years too late to worry about that!'

He tutted gently. 'I don't know—why are you so determined to insult my car? Anybody would think you didn't like me.'

She glared at him again. 'Anybody would be right,' she muttered.

Without warning he swung the car off the road and

screeched to a halt in a lay-by. Abbie was flung forward and grabbed the dashboard automatically, her heart pounding.

'Sorry — the brakes snatch a bit.'

Slowly she released her death-grip on the dashboard and sagged back against the seat. 'Do you always drive like that?' she asked him weakly.

He chuckled softly under his breath. 'Only when I'm trying to impress a woman.'

'I'm impressed,' she groaned. 'Why have we stopped?'

'Because you're telling lies.'

She frowned at him in puzzlement. 'Lies?'

'You said you didn't like me.'

She laughed shortly. 'God, that's some ego you've got.'

His smile was slow and lazy. 'Abbie, Abbie — don't beat around the bush. You like me — even though you might not want to. and you want me — even though you think it's a lousy idea. I do, too, but —— ' His shrug was Gallic and very expressive.

She blushed. 'Dream on,' she muttered.

'Oh, Abigail. You're lovely — but then you know that, don't you?' His fingers sifted through her hair, fanning it out against her shoulders. 'Beautiful — like sunlight trapped in autumn leaves. It feels wonderful. . .' He let it fall from his fingers and sat back with a sigh. 'What's the matter, Abbie? Am I too direct for you? Should I pretend for the sake of convention? Perhaps for the first few days — a fortnight, maybe? Or wait even longer, until you'll believe me if I say I love you, so your conscience is satisfied as well as your body?'

She drew herself away from him, so that the last strand of her hair fell from his fingers, as if breaking the contact would defuse the tension that zinged between them.

He was right, of course. She did like him, and want him, and she did, indeed, think it was a lousy idea. Furthermore, acting on her feelings was the very last thing she intended to do, and she told him so.

'Why?' he asked softly, and his fingers invaded her hair again, sifting the strands with sensuous slowness.

Her heartbeat grew heavier, so that she could feel the blood pulsing through her body, bringing it alive. She pulled away again.

'Are you always so damned unsubtle?'

'Unsubtle? ' He smiled. 'I'm wounded. I thought I was being very understanding.'

She glowered at him. 'I don't know you!'

'There's time.'

'A year. That's all. I'm here for a year.'

He shrugged. 'That's OK. I can handle a long-term relationship.'

'Long-term?' she exclaimed. 'I meant *only* a year!'

He gave a short laugh. 'Damn it, Abbie, I'm not proposing. All I'm suggesting is that we spend some time together — a mutual scratching of itches.'

'I don't do that sort of thing,' she replied tightly, 'and certainly not with egotistical doctors!'

'No? You should. You might enjoy it.'

'I doubt it.'

He shook his head slowly. 'What a waste. Oh, well, if you change your mind, I'm here. We'd better get to the hospice.'

For the rest of the short drive Abbie sat scrunched

up at her side of the car, hardly daring to breathe in case he made some suggestive remark, and wondering all the time how he could possibly have qualified as a doctor when his morals were so clearly askew.

Then she saw him in action at the hospice, and all her preconceptions about him were eroded at a stroke.

They arrived at the modern, purpose-built hospice just as the sun broke through the clouds, and Abbie felt peace steal over her immediately. The buildings were low, constructed in mellow golden brick, and the whole atmosphere was one of tranquillity.

'Lovely, isn't it?' he said softly. 'There are other kinds of healing apart from the physical. It's so easy to forget that, and most hospitals are soulless places, but I love coming here. Every visit refreshes me, even when, as so often, it signals the end. Even so, there's a rightness about it.'

Abbie could feel the rightness seeping into her as they stepped into the airy, quiet reception area.

'Ladies' loo,' he said with a nudge of his head towards a door. 'I'll have a chat to the staff for a minute.'

She escaped gratefully, and hurried back to find him deep in conversation with a diminutive little nurse in sister's uniform.

'You must be Dr Pearce,' she said cheerfully. 'Welcome to St Saviour. We'll look forward to seeing you when Leo comes on his clinic days, shall we?'

She mumbled something non-committal, unaware that Leo even did clinic days at the hospice, and then they left the sister and went towards the little four-bedded ward.

'We're going to see Mary Tanner,' Leo told her.

'She's forty-two, had a mastectomy three years ago and she's got skeletal metastases. Recently she's had some back pain so she's had a course of radiotherapy to try and halt the pressure on the nerves, and she's in for convalescence and drug review before going home again. Lots of emotional problems, obviously. They've got two girls just coming up for their teens.'

They went into the ward, and he was greeted with gentle warmth by the staff, and genuine respect and affection by the patient, Mary Tanner, and her husband Gerry.

He introduced Abbie to them, then perched on the bed and asked Mary how she was feeling now.

'Oh, heaps better. My back feels nearly OK now already and the pain's much better controlled. I feel almost human again,' she said with a low laugh, and Leo smiled.

'Good. Home soon, then?'

'Oh, yes, I think so — if Gerry can cope.'

'Of course I can cope,' he told his wife, but his eyes were sad. Abbie looked away, feeling like an intruder, and Leo stood up to leave, dropping a kiss on Mary's cheek.

'I'll pop in and see you again once you're home. Come with us, Gerry, and we'll have a chat to the staff about when she can leave.'

As they approached the reception area, Leo turned to Gerry. 'How are you really coping?'

He shrugged. 'I just feel so guilty. I've really enjoyed being able to slouch around and take the kids out for long walks without worrying about her, and I feel a real louse because she's the one with the problems, really, and I feel I ought to be offering her more support, but I don't know, I just can't — not all the time. I feel better now, but — oh, I don't know; it's just such hard work trying to be cheerful. . .'

Leo squeezed his shoulder gently. 'Don't feel guilty, Gerry. I'm sure Mary understands, you know — and I think in a way it's a relief for her to have some time away from you all when she doesn't have to be brave and cheerful all the time, too.'

'Really?' He looked doubtful, but was clearly desperate for reassurance, and Leo gave it to him.

'Yes, really. This situation's very emotionally demanding on all of you and you need to recharge your batteries. Once you've done that, you'll be more use to her, and her to you. Don't feel guilty. She'll be home to you soon, and you'll be glad you've had a rest.'

Gerry smiled, more relaxed. 'You're right — as always.'

Leo tapped on the sister's door, and they all trooped in and discussed Mary's progress and decided she should go home at the end of the week unless she had any further set-backs.

As they parted at the door, Gerry turned to Leo and smiled wearily. 'Thanks for dropping by.'

Leo shook his hand warmly. 'My pleasure. See you soon. And don't feel guilty. If you need to talk, you know where to find me.'

Gerry nodded and turned away, walking back to his wife and the crisis in their lives.

'Do you know them well?' Abbie asked, remembering the kiss he had given Mary as they left her bedside.

'No — well, only since Mary's mastectomy. I've spent a lot of time with both of them since. Why?'

She shrugged. 'Just wondered. You kissed her.'

His mouth quirked. 'Jealous, Abbie? The offer's still open.'

So they were back to that, were they? 'Of course I'm not jealous. It just seemed — odd, that's all.'

He shook his head. 'I don't find it odd to greet people with physical contact. I'm a toucher, Abbie. . .'

His hand was resting lightly on the small of her back as he spoke. She stepped away.

'I'd noticed,' she said shortly.

'Whereas you — you're a buttoned-up little virgin.'

'I am not!' she denied hotly, acutely uncomfortable with the sudden shift in the direction of the conversation, and he laughed, a low, smoky laugh that did incredible things to her system.

'Well, then, all I can say is that whoever you've had affairs with didn't even get close to the real you.'

Abbie made no attempt to correct him. What was the point? He was so absolutely right.

CHAPTER TWO

As the days passed, so Abbie's disordered impressions of life in general practice settled down to a sort of pattern.

Peter Sargent, she realised, was the sort to skate through life with cheerful inefficiency, constantly chivvied by the secretarial staff who were quite unmoved by his ingenuous charm.

She discovered that Ravi Patel was single, thirty-four and after Leo, who did precious little to discourage her despite his protestations to the contrary.

As for Leo himself, he was thirty-two and a constant thorn in her side, rattling through his patients at twice the speed of light so that by the time she finally emerged exhausted but triumphant at the end of her surgeries he was long gone on his visits and she was unable to ask him the inevitable string of questions that the consultations had generated.

'Well, you shouldn't dawdle about for so long,' he would tell her, and then would sit and rip through the seemingly knotty problems, so that she felt a complete fool for not having seen the answers herself.

Not that he ever tried to belittle her medical knowledge. He didn't have to. Frankly, she was more than aware of the glaring lapses in her understanding of certain conditions.

As for the paperwork, it defeated her utterly, to the point that when the receptionist told her she should fill in her PC4 she asked where she could find it, much to everyone's amusement.

Leo, not even trying to disguise his mirth, explained cheerfully that a PC4 was a course of four tablets taken as post-coital contraception — hence the name.

Peggy Taylor, the practice manager, took pity on her and told the others off, but it did little to dilute Abbie's humiliation.

It wasn't that she minded being teased — lord, she was used to that. She had two brothers who had taken it as their filial duty to torment the life out of her in her childhood, until, in her teens, she'd suddenly changed into the object of their friends' lascivious attention. Then they'd closed ranks protectively, but even so they still teased her gently to this day.

So it wasn't being teased that troubled her, rather the glaring gaps in her knowledge that the teasing had exposed.

Leo found her later sitting in her surgery surrounded by a heap of textbooks, and came and hitched a lean hip up on to the corner of her desk.

'Boning up on methods of contraception, Abbie?' he teased.

She ignored him huffily.

'Tut-tut,' he admonished. 'Wallowing in self-pity?'

'Oh, go to hell,' she muttered, her voice clogged.

He stuck a finger under her chin and tipped her head up, studying her face intently. She turned away, embarrassed that he should see the traces of tears on her cheeks.

'Leave me alone.'

He stood up, but instead of walking away he came

round her desk, pulled her to her feet and wrapped his
long arms round her.

At first she was stunned into immobility, but after a
few seconds she gave in to the luxury of his undemanding embrace, dropping her head forward into the
hollow of his shoulder and sighing shakily.

His hand came up and smoothed her hair.

'I'm sorry,' he said softly. 'I didn't mean to hurt you,
and I'm sure Jackie didn't.'

'It's not that,' she mumbled into his shirt. 'I just feel
so inadequate. I should have *known* what a PC4 was.'

'Probably,' he agreed, 'but nobody's perfect. Stop
torturing yourself.'

She lifted her head and looked up into his eyes. 'But
what if it's something important? Something life-
threatening, and I don't know about it? I could kill
someone!'

'Do you really think you're that bad?' he asked
quietly. 'Do you really think you would have got so far
in medicine if you were a danger to your patients?'

She gave a shaky laugh. 'Perhaps I just scraped
through—perhaps it was all a fluke. Maybe I just got
the examiners on a good day. Who knows?'

Leo sighed. 'You really don't have a very high
opinion of yourself, do you?'

Numbly, she shook her head. 'There's so much to
know, and I always feel I'm fumbling in the dark. It
terrifies me, Leo, knowing I'm responsible for whether
somebody lives or dies.'

He chuckled. 'In general practice? In the average
week the most drastic thing you're likely to come across
is a nasty case of piles.'

She giggled despite herself. 'You know what I mean.

What if I miss something? What if someone dies because of my ignorance?'

'You can always ask,' he assured her. 'Peter or Ravi or me — any of us. Don't feel you have to cope alone.'

'What about when you've all gone and I'm still here trying to get to grips with this stupid machine?' She flicked a contemptuous glance at the computer, and Leo laughed.

'Does it still hate you?'

'Does it ever,' she grumbled.

'You need a break — have supper with me tonight.'

She realised she was still standing in his arms, although she wasn't crushed up against him any more, but she might just as well have been because she could feel the warmth of his body, could remember the feel of it, long and hard and lean, all sleek, solid muscle and sinew, terrifyingly, overwhelming male.

She stepped back a little further. 'I don't think that would be a good idea,' she said as firmly as she could manage.

'Why?'

'I — I just don't. . .' she floundered.

His grin was wicked. 'Not good enough. Come on, you've finished here for the night.'

He flicked off her terminal, stacked her books back on to the shelf and held out his hand. 'Come.'

'What if I don't want to?' she said defensively.

He sighed. 'You're lying again, Abbie,' he teased in a soft, sing-song voice.

Her mouth firmed in defiance. 'I have to study.'

'Cobblers,' he said rudely. 'Come on. We'll pick up a take-away.'

Her stomach rumbled loudly at the thought, and he chuckled. 'Co-operation at last!'

'Only from my involuntary muscles——'

'That'll do for a start. I realise that aggravating mouth of yours will take a little longer to tame. Come on—and say, Yes, Leo.'

She sighed. 'Yes, Leo.'

'Better. Now come on.'

She assumed they'd have fish and chips, or a Chinese at the outside, but the little town surprised her. Tucked away in a narrow alley off the main street was a tiny but immaculate kebab house owned and run by a Greek Cypriot who, Leo said, had come over from Cyprus at the time of the Turkish invasion in the early seventies and stayed ever since.

The shop, predictably, was called Spiro's, and Spiro himself was almost circular, balding and grumbled constantly about the price of lamb and the rubbish at the market.

Leo, commiserating, bought shish kebabs in pitta pockets groaning with salad, and they ate them in the car looking out over a field because they were both too hungry to wait any longer. Despite Spiro's complaints the quality was superb, and Abbie ate every last bit and even pinched a bit of Leo's second one.

Then he drove her back to his house, a cottage on a quiet lane about two miles from the town centre, and the evening sun gleamed on the windows and on the glowing banks of perennials that flanked the path, the magenta of the crane's bill, the green and white of the lady's-mantle, the tall spires of the hollyhocks nodding at the back behind the white and yellow daisies.

'Oh, how pretty!' Abbie said, enchanted, and Leo

let them in, retrieved a bottle of wine and two glasses and took her for a stroll round the garden.

The evening was much cooler than the day had been, and she was able to enjoy the mellow air and the sweetly scented roses that graced the soft pink walls.

'How do you manage it all?' she asked, incredulous, after he had finished his guided tour.

He laughed softly. 'Me? I wouldn't know a dandelion from a primula! I have a gardener who comes in twice a week and cuts the grass and keeps the beds in order.'

'He does a wonderful job,' she said admiringly, glancing round again at the riot of colour that filled every corner.

'She. Yes, she's excellent, I have to say. When I moved here the garden was a mess, but she's worked wonders.'

'She?' Abbie said with a teasing grin. 'I might have known.'

'Of course. She's tall, blonde and very, very lovely.' He grinned back. 'She's also in her late forties and a grandmother. I swear she's stronger than I am, and she's definitely no competition to you, Abigail, my love, so you needn't get all jealous.'

She looked away hastily. 'I'm not your love, Leo, and I don't intend to be. And I'm *certainly* not jealous!' She glanced at her watch. 'Look, I really ought to get on. I've got studying I should be doing, and I'm sure you've got better things to do ——'

He laughed softly. 'Running, Abbie?'

'Not at all,' she blustered, but she was, and they both knew it.

He took pity on her, though, and drove her back to the surgery so that she could collect her car.

As she unlocked the door, she became suddenly, startlingly aware of his body close behind her. His hand, warm and hard, closed over her shoulder and turned her gently towards him.

'Leo?' she said breathlessly, and then her protest, such as it was, was cut off by his lips as they covered hers in a feather-light caress.

'Goodnight, Abigail,' he murmured softly, and then he turned on his heel and walked back to his car.

Shaken, she unlocked her door and slid behind the wheel, her limbs trembling. He was waiting for her to start the car and drive away, she thought dimly, so mechanically she turned the key, backed out and drove off.

After a moment she realised he was flashing his lights furiously at her, and she pulled over.

He leapt out of his car and ran towards her. She wound down the window just far enough to talk to him but not so far that he could kiss her again — just in case.

'What do you want?' she asked nervously.

'Me? That's an interesting thought.'

'Leo——'

'You didn't have your lights on.'

She blinked. 'Oh — right. Thanks.'

His grin was infuriating. 'My pleasure. I didn't realise one little kiss would throw you so badly.'

'It's nothing to do with your kiss!' she protested, and the grin widened.

'You're telling porkie-pies again, Abbie, darling,' he murmured, and, slipping his hand through the partly-open window, he brushed her cheek with his knuckles.

It sent a shiver through her, as did his softly voiced, 'Sleep well, princess. Dream of me.'

She closed her eyes. 'Leo, go away,' she said unsteadily, but he was gone, leaving her in a tangle of wild and unfamiliar emotions, not least of which was a most unsettling feeling that she would, indeed, be dreaming of him — with or without his permission!

She didn't dream of him, in the end — largely because she didn't sleep until almost dawn, because every time she closed her eyes she felt the brush of lips on hers and her whole body screamed to life.

Unable to bear it, incapable of sweeping aside such unfamiliar and overwhelming sensations, she paced her little flat over a shoe-shop in the centre of town and wondered how she was going to get through the next year.

By ignoring him whenever possible, was the conclusion she eventually came to, and after a drink of hot milk and another severe lecture to herself she finally crawled exhausted into bed shortly before dawn to fall instantly and deeply asleep until the traffic woke her at almost eight-thirty.

Predictably, she was late, and, equally predictably, her surgery was less than straightforward. To add insult to injury, she found that when under pressure the computer was even less co-operative, and she finally, in desperation, asked Peggy if she could come in and sit with her and show her what she was doing wrong.

'No,' Peggy told her, 'I don't think the patients would like it, but Leo's here. I'll send him in; it'll get him off my back while I type these letters.'

Seconds later there was a tap on the door and Leo

appeared clutching two cups of coffee and the computer manual.

'Problems?'

'It hates me!' she wailed despairingly.

He chuckled. 'Nonsense. It's an inanimate object. It's incapable of hate.'

'Oh, yeah?' she snorted. 'Tell it to the fairies.' She glanced at him, took in the cool cotton trousers and the turned-back cuffs of his shirt, exposing strong, hair-strewn wrists, and turned quickly away. After that kiss the night before, the very last thing she needed was him beside her looking sexy as all get-out. She forced herself to concentrate. 'Look, how do I recall previous prescriptions and history?' she asked, her voice a little strained to her ears.

Leo, apparently oblivious to her discomfort, leant over her, his body brushing hers, casually tapping buttons, and the information on her next patient appeared as if by magic. She blinked. The vital manoeuvres were still lost to her, drowned out by the clamouring of her hormones.

'How did you do that?' she asked faintly.

He grinned. 'Easy—you should have watched.'

'I did,' she lied. 'It takes me ages to get it to do that, and I'm sure I go through a far longer process—— Right, show me again.'

He shook his head. 'Finish your surgery and I'll go over it with you afterwards. I'll just sit here and help you get through the rest of your patients for now.'

One or two of the patients looked askance at Leo, but he smilingly explained that they were having problems with the computer and he was fighting with it to try and save the patients' waiting time.

'Just ignore me,' he said, but Abbie found it intensely off-putting and difficult.

Until, that was, she had a patient with a seemingly innocent mole just below her collarbone. She examined it, asked all the appropriate questions and was on the point of telling the patient to go home and stop worrying when Leo's toe connected none too gently with her ankle.

She glanced at him, but he was staring fixedly at the computer screen. She followed the direction of his eyes, and saw 'Excision and histology' on the screen.

She cleared her throat, smiled at the patient and shot up some thanks for Leo's presence at her elbow. 'Right,' she told the patient, 'what we need to do is remove it, just as a precaution, and then send it to the lab to have it checked, just to be on the safe side. I'm sure it's nothing to worry about, but removing it is such a minor procedure it seems silly not to do so. Now, the only thing is I'm not an expert in minor surgery, but I believe Dr Chandler here could remove it for you, couldn't you, Dr Chandler?'

He turned a charming smile on the young woman. 'My pleasure,' he murmured, and he told her to book in with the receptionist for surgery the following day. 'Dr Pearce will, of course, assist me and continue with your follow-up,' he added, and the woman smiled gratefully at both of them and left.

Abbie turned to Leo. 'Is it really necessary to remove it?' she asked, her confidence shaken yet again.

He shrugged. 'Probably not, but it's the sort of blemish that could easily turn into melanoma, if not now then in the future, and it's so dead easy to take them off and check. We have a set procedure, by the way, for follow-up of any mole or skin lesion removed in the surgery. All material excised is sent for histology, always, without exception, and the patient is always recalled automatically when the result comes back because if they've gone to the lengths of consulting their doctor they're going to worry till they know the answer one way or the other. The only time we don't do it ourselves is if we're sure it's gone too far for simple excision or in the case of a difficult site.'

'Difficult as in cosmetically difficult?'

'Or in one of the areas where nerves are likely to be implicated, like the anterior triangle of the neck, or eyelids, or over the flexor tendons of the fingers, for instance. Cheeks can be difficult, too, both cosmetically and because of the nerves and glands over the jaws. We do what we can, but it's important to know your limitations. We aren't plastic surgeons, and some procedures require other skills.'

'What about this lady?' Abbie asked doubtfully. 'Won't she have some scarring?'

He grinned wryly. 'No faith, have you? I'm not a complete butcher, Abbie. She might have a tiny scar, but I won't disfigure her for life, my love. Right, who's next?'

Abbie, completely fazed by his endearment, floundered on with her surgery until all her patients had been dealt with and the computer had gobbled up Leo's instructions, obediently spewed out various prescriptions and gone quietly back to sleep.

She glared at it. 'I don't know how you do it,' she grumbled crossly. 'Horrid thing.'

Leo grinned. 'Think of the writer's cramp it's saved you.'

She snorted. 'Yes, I've got cramp of the brain instead!'

'All comes of being a simple-minded woman——'

'It's nothing to do with——' she began, rising instantly to the bait, but then, seeing his dancing eyes, she subsided immediately. 'Thank you so much for your help,' she said instead, batting her lashes at him.

He laughed. 'Come on, time for visits. Mary Tanner has gone home and I have to pop in and see her. Want to come?'

'Sure. How's her husband coping?' she asked as she packed up her things.

'I don't know. That's one of the things I want to find out.'

She followed him out, returning the patient envelopes to the office as she went.

Predictably, Peggy was waiting with a question. 'Did you mean to send this urine off on a haematology form?'

'Oh, hell,' she muttered.

Behind her Leo tutted and gave a resigned sigh while she quickly filled in the correct form and gave it to the patient practice manager.

'Sorry, Peggy,' she said with an apologetic smile, and was greeted with an encouraging pat on the hand.

'Don't worry, it'll come with time.'

'I wish,' she muttered under her breath, and then Leo was wheeling her out of the door and towards the car.

'Now, do you need the loo before we go?' he asked with heavy tolerance, and she glared at him.

'No, thank you.'

'Sure?'

'Perfectly!'

'Don't get grotty with me——'

'I'm not getting grotty!' she said, her voice rising steadily.

He tutted again. 'You'll be stamping your foot in a second.' He hopped over the door and slid behind the wheel, watching with interest as Abbie struggled into the low bucket seat, her skirt riding up as she did so.

She shot him a furious glare. 'Don't leer,' she told him crossly. 'And anyway, where's your Volvo? Isn't it time you got it back?'

'All in good time—anyway, I get a better view of your legs in Topsy.'

She glowered at him, and he chuckled. 'God, you're gorgeous when you're angry, do you know that?'

She looked hastily away. 'Where are we going?'

'To see Mary Tanner, then an elderly lady with congestive heart failure who's struggling for breath. I've put her on Bambuterol but I want to see if it's doing the trick.'

'I haven't heard of it,' Abbie said, and then could have kicked herself.

'Now, why doesn't that surprise me?' he murmured. 'In fact, I wouldn't have expected you to, because it's pretty new. It's a bronchodilator like Ventolin, but oral, to give her more prophylactic cover over twenty-four hours. She's been waking up breathless and in those circumstances an inhaler is a bit like shutting the stable door after the horse has bolted. Anyway, we'll see if it's working. Right, here we go.'

The engine purred smoothly to life, and Leo swung the car out on to the road and headed for the Tanners' house while Abbie tried to appear nonchalant, hold her hair down and keep her knees out of reach all at once.

She failed — at least with the knees. As the car swerved round a corner, so she slid over the leather upholstery and fetched up against the gear lever just as Leo reached for it.

With a gasp she swivelled out of reach but not before the touch of his warm fingers had sent shivers down her spine. He threw her a teasing grin.

'If you want me to touch you, Abbie, you only have to ask,' he said softly, and his voice, deep and gravelly, turned her bones to jelly and her resolve to mush.

'You should be so lucky,' she mumbled, and let go of her hair to get a firmer grip on the seat. 'Of course, if you weren't going round the corners like a bat out of hell I wouldn't slide around so much.'

'Your bottom's too small. If you had a few curves, you'd fit the seat better,' he replied with a grin.

'I have curves,' she told him primly.

His eyes slid over her body and back to the road. 'I'd noticed — but only on the front.'

Abbie's top-heaviness had been the bane of her adolescence. All gangly legs and boyishly slim hips, the last thing she had expected or wanted was the lush fullness of her breasts, which had appeared as if by magic when she was thirteen and kept growing out of all proportion to her otherwise streamlined frame. Her brothers had ragged her to death about it, and so she had acquired a complex about a mile wide. As she grew older she had learned to deal with the leers of her male colleagues, and by wearing loose blouses and jackets she had managed to minimise the problem.

Not, apparently, enough to fool Leo. She felt the

blush coming and turned away so that he wouldn't see, but they were at the end of their journey and he pulled up outside the Tanners' house and turned to her.

'Coming in?'

'Only if you'll stop this endless sexual harassment,' she told him grimly.

He stopped in the act of climbing out of the car and turned back to her, her face serious for once. 'Abbie, I'm only teasing.'

'Are you?' She made herself look at him. 'What about all this rubbish about an affair? Is that teasing, too?'

He met her eyes for a long time, the gold flecks gleaming in their blue surround, making his eyes almost green—like a lion, she thought, predatory but content to watch—for now. She licked her lips. 'Well?' she prompted.

'No, that isn't teasing. I'm more than ready for anything you want to offer. Just say the word. For the rest——' He shrugged. 'You take youself too seriously.'

'Damn it, Leo, someone has to! I'm sick of being treated like a bimbo just because I've got——' She floundered to a halt.

'A chest like a page-three model?'

She flushed furiously and turned away. 'Exactly. Female exploitation.'

He chuckled. 'Oh, come on, Abbie—I've seen you looking at me. If you'd only admit it was mutual we'd maybe stand a chance.'

'No way.'

He sighed and finished climbing out of the car. 'Coming?'

She opened the door, grabbed her skirt and yanked

it down as she squirmed out of the seat. As she straightened, she met his eyes and the blue and gold burned bright like a hot flame. The sun glinted on his tawny hair, and he stood quite still, watching her. She felt frozen by his eyes, pinned to the spot, unable to move or look away. He reminded her of a big cat, a lion, relaxed but ready to spring—on her.

She had the distinct feeling that with this particular lion, though, her time was running out. He wasn't going to be content to watch for much longer—and she felt about as defenceless as a new-born lamb.

CHAPTER THREE

GERRY TANNER greeted them at the door, and Abbie thought his face seemed less drawn than the first time she had seen him.

'Hi,' he said with a smile. 'Come in. Mary's in the garden at the moment, sunning herself. Can I get you a drink?'

'Something cold?' Leo asked hopefully, and Mr Tanner nodded.

'I made some fresh lemonade this morning for Mary—will that do?'

Abbie couldn't think of anything more wonderful. It was another scorcher, with the August sun beating relentlessly down on them, and she was desperate for some cool retreat. She found it, moments later, when they left Gerry Tanner getting the drinks and Leo led her through the house and out of the patio doors at the back into the garden.

It was a lovely little oasis, cool and leafy, and they found Mary under a tree on a swinging hammock, fast asleep.

Leo touched her gently on the hand, and her eyes flew open.

She propped herself up on one elbow and smiled self-consciously. 'Sorry—I must have dropped off.'

Leo returned the smile. 'Don't apologise. I'm not surprised you were asleep, it's so peaceful here.' He picked up the book that had fallen on to the lawn, and glanced at the cover. 'It must be riveting,' he said drily.

Mary laughed. 'Actually, it is, but I'm finding it difficult to concentrate with the pain-killers.'

She was on a sustained release oral diamorphine, with Maxalon to alleviate the sickness she was suffering as a result, but at least she was kept relatively pain-free. Leo settled himself on a nearby garden chair and eyed his patient thoughtfully.

'So, how do you feel?'

'Physically?'

'That'll do for a start.'

Mary shrugged. 'Oh, the pain's better and I'm not feeling nearly so sick, but I still feel so weak — frustrated, really, sums it up. I just can't seem to do anything, and I've never sat still in my life. The garden's getting full of weeds, and there are some shrubs I meant to put in over there but I just haven't got round to it.'

'I don't think you ought to flagellate yourself with guilt, Mary,' Leo told her, his face grave. 'There are more important things in life than whether a few pounds' worth of shrubs get put in.'

Mary sighed raggedly. 'Oh, it's not just that. I wouldn't see them flower anyway, so I can't get excited about it, but I meant to decorate the girls' rooms last summer, and I just didn't get round to it. I don't know — you always think you can do it tomorrow, and now it's too late because there won't be any tomorrows, and there just seems to be so much I've left undone. I thought I'd have more time. . .'

Abbie wanted to weep for her, for her frustration

and anger, for her guilt, for all she left unsaid, but above all for the untimely end that drew ever nearer.

Leo, too, was clearly touched by her sorrow. He asked, very quietly, 'How are you getting on with Gerry and the girls?'

'Oh, not brilliantly, you know — he still doesn't seem to want to accept the fact that I'm dying, and the girls just avoid the subject all the time. I just wish someone would acknowledge it so I could talk to them about their future!'

Leo shook his head. 'Perhaps they just don't know how to talk to you about it.'

She shrugged again. 'I just feel — I don't know — cut off, I suppose. As if it isn't happening to me, and no one will give me the chance to talk about it, to say the things I need to say.'

'Such as?'

'Oh — well, that I'm sorry for the things I've done that have annoyed them over the years, that I've forgiven them for things they've done — that I love them. I don't know. I want to give Gerry a foolproof list of instructions for bringing up the girls, and I want to answer all their questions before they even occur to them to ask, and I want to be sure that they're equipped for the world. It's such a ghastly place, and I don't know how they'll cope. . . Basically I think I just want to leave everything in order before I say goodbye, but I don't know how to start.'

Leo leaned across and squeezed her hand. 'Everyone's different, but we all have our own way of coping. Some of us are just better at it than others, and at the moment Gerry's way of coping is denial. Don't worry, I'll try and talk to him and see if I can help him come to terms with it so you can talk to each other and say all the things that need to be said.'

She sighed shakily. 'I don't know if I'll be able to do it—not when the crunch comes.'

'You will,' Leo assured her softly. 'When the time comes, you'll find the way—and if you still can't there are plenty of people available who can help you to start talking to each other about it.'

Mary gazed wistfully across the garden for a while, then turned back to them with a sigh. 'I think Gerry's angry with me for leaving him.'

'I expect he is. He doesn't want to be a widower in his forties with the responsibility for bringing up two young girls.'

Mary gave a lop-sided grin. 'I'm not exactly ecstatic about it myself!'

Leo's mouth softened in a gentle smile of understanding. 'No—no, I imagine you aren't, but for you at least dying will be the end of the road. For them, in many ways, it's just the beginning, and that's bound to be frightening. Fear often makes us angry.'

Abbie watched as Mary's face became pensive. 'I don't know how they'll cope.'

'We'll be here for them—they can talk to the staff at the hospice, and all the staff at our practice are at their disposal. They know that. All of us are able to help with practical as well as emotional issues, and the social services are very good. What about your solicitor?'

'He's a friend—he's got everything under control, so there shouldn't be anything left to chance. Hopefully he'll have everything sorted out quickly on the money side—let's face it, Gerry's an accountant so he should be able to cope with it. He's a very good coper, aren't you, darling?' she added for Gerry's benefit, just as he arrived with the drinks.

'Oh, brilliant,' he said lightly, but there were lines of strain round his eyes and Abbie could tell he was only coping with difficulty.

Leo, to Abbie's surprise, was extraordinarily sensitive to his mood and gave him plenty of opportunity to talk about his feelings. It was clear, though, that he didn't feel able to discuss them, and so after a few more general questions Leo stood up, gesturing to Abbie to do the same.

'Could you see us out, Gerry?' he asked softly, and the man nodded. In the hall, Leo turned to him. 'Why don't you come in and have a chat with us one day when someone's here with Mary? Go through some of the things that are troubling you, see if we can find some answers?'

For a second fear flickered in his eyes, and Abbie's kind heart reached out to him. How frightening it must be to have no certainty any more.

Then he nodded, and the fear was joined by relief. Clearly he needed to talk to someone—just not his wife.

They took their leave, and Abbie sat quietly in the car, absorbing her impressions. She had, of course, dealt with the problem of death both imminent and recent in her work in the hospital, but it was the first time she had been exposed to the process of two people coming to terms with the changes it would make in their lives, and she felt both moved and privileged.

'OK?' Leo asked as she slid into the low seat. For once his eyes were on her face, not her legs, and she nodded briefly.

'Yes, I suppose so. It's just. . .'

'Sad?' he offered.

'Mmm. Terribly. I wonder how they will cope.'

Leo started the car and pulled away. 'God knows. Badly, I suspect. Most people do. Right, Mrs Willis.'

They crossed the little town and pulled up outside a row of tiny terraced houses. Mrs Willis lived in the middle one, with tatty net curtains at the window and a weedy, untended little front garden. It was in direct contrast to the Tanners' house, and Abbie fully expected their patient to be small, frail and weak. Instead the door was opened by a very obese woman, puffing and blowing, her cheeks reddened and her lips slightly bluish.

'Hello there,' Leo said cheerfully. 'I've brought Dr Pearce with me — she's with the practice for a while to find out if she fancies being a GP, so I'm just showing her the ropes. OK?'

'Of course — come in, dear,' Mrs Willis wheezed, and they followed her as she waddled down the narrow passage to the back room. Abbie wrinkled her nose. There was an overwhelming smell of unwashed body and boiled cod, heavily overlaid with stale cigarette smoke, and she felt her stomach rebelling.

'You'll have to excuse the mess; can't get about like I used to,' Mrs Willis wheezed by way of explanation.

Abbie, following Leo into the room, nearly gagged.

It was chaotic, the table strewn with what looked like last week's plates — even the cat asleep on the bed in the corner had disdained the left-overs. The ashtray was overflowing, and empty cigarette packets were strewn around the brimming waste-paper basket.

Leo glanced round and shook his head. 'All too

much for you now, isn't it? Why don't I see if I can organise a home help for you?'

She coughed, a harsh, wheezy, bronchitic cough, and Abbie helped her into the only vacant chair. The other was heaped with clothes, and there was nowhere for them to sit, so she stood back and watched Leo at work again.

Would he say anything about the smoking? she wondered. Clearly it was doing Mrs Willis no good at all, but, if she was still smoking heavily at the age of seventy-odd, she wasn't about to stop because a doctor advised it, Abbie was sure.

She was right. Mrs Willis gave a rueful smile and patted his hand. 'I know what you're going to say, but it's no good, Doctor; I can't seem to do without the weed.'

Leo pursed his lips pensively. 'Did you try the patches?'

'Bah!' she spat. 'Patches? Ain't no good to me, Doctor—I need something to do with my hands!'

'Knitting?' Abbie suggested. 'When my mother gave up, she started knitting us all jumpers. They were dreadful, but none of us had the heart to say so. By the time she realised, she didn't need to keep her hands busy any more!'

Mrs Willis gave a wheezy chuckle. 'I tried that, dear, and believe me, my family told me what they thought! No, I'm stuck with it, I'm afraid, so you'll just have to do the best you can with me. Sorry!'

Leo grunted agreement, and, tucking his stethoscope into his ears, he ferreted about among the endless layers of grubby underwear to listen to Mrs Willis's chest.

'How are your ankles?' he asked, kneeling down to feel for oedema around the base of her shins.

'Oh, a bit puffy, but wouldn't you be, dragging this lot around?'

The room filled with her wheezy laugh again, and Abbie found herself warming to the woman. All right, she was smelly and the place was chaotic, and in a way it was probably self-inflicted, but even so she had a lovely, bubbly personality and the precious ability to laugh at herself which Abbie found very appealing.

Nevertheless, she was glad to get out in the fresh air again.

Their route back to the surgery took them along the high street where Abbie's flat was, and on impulse she suggested they stop for lunch.

Leo's brows shot up, and she immediately regretted her stupidity, but it was too late to change her mind. He parked quite close to the shoe-shop, picked up his medical bag and followed her through the door and up the steep stairs between the shops to the little flat above.

It was airless and stuffy, so she flung open the windows in the little sitting-room and went through to the kitchen. The window stuck, however, and she turned to call Leo just as he reached over.

'Allow me,' he murmured, and, stretching one arm above her head, he tugged the sash down.

'Thank you,' she said a trifle breathlessly, and looked quickly away from those flashing blue-gold eyes.

She found herself staring at a large expanse of shirt, draped softly over a lean, hard chest that rose and fell evenly just inches from her nose. She swallowed. Thick, golden hair curled against the base of his throat in the open V of his shirt. It looked incredibly soft, and she wondered idly if it was as soft as it looked, or if it would chafe against her bare skin. . .

He was still, motionless, and she felt as if she was caught in time, like a fly trapped in amber.

Then his hand fell from the window and she felt his fingers, long and lean and hard, threading through her hair and drawing her head back.

'Abigail,' he murmured, and then his mouth closed over hers with the smallest of sighs, and she was lost.

His other hand came up and rested on her spine, easing her against him, and the contrast of his lean, rangy frame against her softer one was like coming home.

She made a tiny contented sound and he drew her closer, deepening the kiss as he did so. She felt the trembling start in her knees and spread up through the rest of her body, and she slid her arms up round his neck and clung tighter.

With a ragged groan he lifted his head. 'Where's the bedroom?' he asked gruffly.

Common sense returned like a bucketful of cold water, and as she took in his burning eyes, the flush lying on his cheekbones, the soft fullness of his mouth she closed her eyes and moaned, turning away.

'No, Leo,' she whispered, thoroughly shaken by his reaction as well as her own.

'Oh, come on, Abbie, don't play games with me —'

'I'm not playing games!' she protested unsteadily. 'Leo, I never meant. . .'

'Then why are we here? Why did you invite me here?'

'For lunch,' she said desperately. 'Only for lunch!'

He turned her face back towards him, and stared long and hard into her eyes before sighing and releasing her.

'You're either the most appalling tease or far too naïve for your own good,' he said eventually, his voice hard. 'Which is it, Abbie?'

She dropped her head on to her chest, ashamed of her stupidity. Of course he had read more into her invitation—was she mad to think he wouldn't? Damn it, he'd been after her for days. Only a complete idiot would have invited the lion in for a meal and not expected to be on the menu!

'I'm sorry,' she mumbled. 'I didn't mean to lead you on. I'm just not very good at this sort of thing.'

'What sort of thing, Abbie? Playing cat and mouse with someone's feelings?'

Her head whipped up. 'I wasn't! Really, Leo, I just meant lunch —— Oh, hell, can we go, please?'

His face softened, the desire still there but joined now by humour. 'You mean I don't even get lunch either now?'

She swallowed. 'It's only cheese ——'

'That'll do fine.'

She went towards the fridge, but his long arms snaked out and drew her gently against his chest.

'How about another kiss first?'

'Leo ——'

Her protest was cut off by his lips, and she closed her eyes, slid her arms round his waist and gave up fighting.

The kiss, however, was short-lived, and this time it was Leo who pulled back.

'Lunch,' he said softly, and she almost fell when he let her go and wandered off into the sitting-room.

Aroused, confused and ashamed of her silliness, she fiddled with the cheese and biscuits for ages, until Leo came back in and stood in the doorway, watching her thoughtfully.

'Um—it's ready,' she mumbled, and his mouth tilted in a knowing smile.

'Good—I'm starving,' he told her, but she had the distinct feeling it wasn't cheese and biscuits he wanted!

She opened a carton of apple juice and put two plates on the table, and then realised that the table was tiny and no matter where she sat she would be almost certain to touch him.

Still smiling that knowing smile, he lowered himself on to one of the chairs and stretched his legs out sideways. Gratefully she tucked hers under the table and then was confounded when he swung his legs round and trapped her feet between his.

'Aren't you a little old to play footsie under the table?' she said in her best school-marm voice, and he chuckled.

'Don't be boring. What's this?'

'Sage Derby, and don't change the subject. I want my feet back.'

He released them, and she had to resist the urge to tuck them under her bottom out of his way. His eyes were harder to avoid, gleaming with laughter and more besides—a remnant of heat that unsettled her and put her off her food.

'What about Mrs Willis?' she asked, desperate to take both her mind and Leo's off the subject of their mutual attraction.

'What about Mrs Willis?'

'Is there honestly anything you can do for her?'

He shrugged and settled back in the chair. 'Not really. I can get her a home help, but she's thirty years too late to get a grip on her lifestyle. She needs to lose about five stone, give up smoking and totally change her eating habits, but I'm afraid it's a cast of locking the stable door after the horse has bolted.'

Abbie agreed. By now the damage was done, but she didn't like to think there was nothing they could do.

'Don't you run a weight clinic in the surgery?'

He nodded. 'Oh, yes, but she can't get out any more so she couldn't come. We also run a smoking clinic, but the same applies. No, I'm sorry to have to admit defeat, but at this stage all we can do is alleviate her symptoms to a greater or lesser degree. Really, it's just a holding operation.'

'Poor Mrs Willis,' Abbie sighed.

Leo looked surprised. 'I thought you'd hate her.'

'Why?'

He shrugged. 'She stinks, she's idle and won't help herself—nobody else in the practice will go near her if they can avoid it. She's actually Ravinda's patient, but she can't bear her.'

'Figures.'

'Ooo. You really don't get on with Ravi, do you?'

Abbie chuckled. 'Would you expect me to? I'm just the hired help, Leo—hardly more than a student.'

He pursed his lips and leant back. 'Have you got over your feelings of inadequacy yet?'

'About general practice? Not really. I'm still terrified every time I have to make a decision.'

'It'll come with time. You haven't made any howlers yet, I don't think.'

'I nearly did today—if you hadn't been there that girl with the mole would have gone home untreated.'

'And probably been none the worse for it. Still, it'll come off tomorrow and then we'll know.' He reached out a lazy hand and popped a chunk of cheese in his mouth. 'I like this Sage Derby.'

'Good. Cup of tea?'

He shook his head. 'We ought to get back—much as I'd like to linger. . .'

One look at his eyes and Abbie was immediately galvanised into action.

She had a nasty, sneaking feeling that it was simply, like Mrs Willis's treatment, a holding operation and that sooner or later he was going to pounce.

Probably sooner. . .

The following day Lorraine Creasey, the girl with the mole, came back to have it excised, and Abbie had her first experience of minor surgery in general practice.

Because they were some distance from a hospital the practice handled quite a lot of minor surgical cases, Leo told her, and she was fascinated to see the little room they had set aside especially for it. Miss Creasey, the patient, was a little nervous at first but Abbie wasn't surprised to see Leo set her at her ease within seconds.

He was such a natural communicator, she acknowledged, although he certainly didn't waste time in idle chit-chat. Assisted by the practice nurse, he worked fast, efficiently and without any unnecessary movements, and he was a joy to observe.

During her training Abbie had worked with several surgeons, so she was able to appreciate Leo's precise and delicate technique. There would be little or no scarring, she was sure, unless Lorraine was very unlucky.

'Right,' he said after it was all finished, 'we'll send everything we've removed for analysis at the lab as a precaution, but it all looks very innocuous.'

The young woman's smile was one of genuine relief. 'I'm so glad. I thought I was making a fuss about nothing, but there's been such a lot of it in the news, it's just nice to be reassured.'

Leo grinned easily. 'That's what we're here for,' he told her. 'We'll be in touch as soon as we have the results. If you haven't heard from us by the end of next week, ring up. OK?'

'Fine — thanks.'

Abbie watched her go. 'She batted her eyelashes at you,' she teased.

'Jealous, Abbie?' he teased back.

She snorted. 'Modesty isn't your greatest failing, is it?'

Sue, the practice nurse, chuckled. 'They all bat their eyelashes at him, Abbie. You'll soon get used to it. Brocklingford's greatest hearthrob, aren't you, Leo? Going to break a few hearts tonight?'

'That's me. What are you doing tonight, Sue?'

'Making tea for my husband and sons — what are you doing, Abbie?'

'Studying,' she said firmly.

'Really?' Leo frowned. 'You can do too much.'

She snorted. 'I doubt that. Anyway, what's the choice? I doubt if you'll be doing anything that dynamic,' she added without thinking, and could have kicked herself.

'I don't know.' He shot her an enquiring glance. 'I shall probably be lying in the garden with a book—unless I get a better offer?'

'Take a hike,' she told him candidly, and Sue chuckled again.

'That's it, Abbie—put him in his place. Too much admiration isn't good for him.'

Leo snorted. 'Chance'd be a fine thing,' he muttered, labelling up the last of the samples for histology. 'Right, Sue, could you drop these off in Reception for me? Abbie and I have a training session booked.'

'We have?'

'We have.'

'Since when?' she asked indignantly.

'About thirty seconds ago—come on, don't keep me waiting. I'm a doctor—you should never keep a doctor waiting; they're important people, second only to God.'

Sue laughed. 'You put yourself that far down the list, Leo? Someone must have been at your ego recently.'

He chucked a soggy paper towel at her and led Abbie from the room. 'Ignore her—rude woman. Now, let's go in my surgery—it's cooler than yours—and we'll have a look at a few cases.'

'Not more amateur dramatics?' Abbie pleaded, but he was unmoved.

'Do you good to let your hair down. Right.' He shut the door of his surgery behind them and pushed Abbie towards his chair behind the desk, taking the patient's seat beside it. 'I'm Mr X, I'm thirty-nine years old and I've just come in and told you I've got stomach pains.'

He looked at her expectantly, and she rolled her eyes. 'Leo, I hate this — can't we just discuss the case without playing make-believe?'

'It's very valuable. Come on.'

She sighed. 'All right, Mr X — tell me where it hurts.'

'Sort of all over — like stabbing pains, sometimes.'

'Before or after you eat?'

'Well — I don't know, really.'

'Fat lot of help you are,' Abbie snorted, and Leo tutted.

'Stay in role, Abbie, dear.'

'Don't "Abbie dear" me — this is a waste of time. What's wrong with you?'

He chuckled. 'You're the doctor — you tell me!'

'You're malingering and trying to get attention,' she told him firmly. 'I suggest you go home and pull yourself together.'

'No, that's the pair of curtains, not the stomach ache. I heard another one today — Doctor, help me, I've swallowed my mouth organ. Good job you don't play the piano, son!'

Abbie groaned and then giggled. 'You're incorrigible.'

'I try to be. I tell you what, I'll let you off this training session on one condition — let me get you dinner.'

'How did I know there'd be a catch?' she sighed.

'Well?'

'Anything to get out of another role-play exercise!' she laughed.

He grinned. 'You won't regret it — I'm a good cook.'

Too late she realised he meant to cook for her — and she would be trapped with him in his little cottage, unable to escape, with nothing but the shreds of her resolve to keep them apart.

Was she strong enough? God alone knows, she thought, and her heart danced crazily against her ribs.

But whether with fear or anticipation she was unable to decide. . .

CHAPTER FOUR

ABBIE dressed conservatively—nothing too delicate or feminine, nothing provocative, just clean, simple lines that minimised the impact of her curves and—hopefully—reduced her appeal. The shirt was sand-washed silk, soft and comfortable, in a lovely jade-green that reflected her eyes, and she wore it with a pair of tailored culottes in a darker green and flat leather sandals because heels made her legs look even longer. The legs themselves she left bare because the evening was still warm and she couldn't bear the thought of tights.

She also put her hair up, skewering it firmly to her head so that it couldn't blow around when she went in his car—and coincidentally so that there was no opportunity for him to run his fingers through it and torment her!

Finished, she stood back and surveyed herself, well-satisfied with the result. She looked cool, pleasant and very normal—not at all the sort of thing that would turn Leo on! Excellent. Effort well spent, she decided.

Her effort was wasted. Leo took one look at her and smiled, a lazy, satisfied smile. 'You look delectable,' he told her, and she scowled, to his amusement. 'You really ought to learn to accept compliments graciously,' he tutted.

She sniffed disdainfully, and he chuckled. 'You can't disguise it, Abbie—you're beautiful—warm, soft, all woman. Putting your hair up——' he teased the tendrils round her nape with long, knowing fingers '—won't take that away—and that wonderfully soft, sensuous silk shirt would be better belted in to that tiny little waist of yours.' His fingers trailed down over the buttons and settled against her hip, imitating the belt. 'It doesn't show off your figure properly—or is that the idea?'

Cross because he had caught her out, she turned, grim-lipped, and elbowed him out of the way to lock her door behind them.

'Don't be grouchy just because I appreciate you,' he said softly in her ear, and she cursed the shiver that ran over her skin where his breath had brushed so lightly.

'I am not grouchy,' she said grouchily, even crosser now.

He laughed, a low, sensuous sound in the little recess by the door, curling round her and teasing her senses.

It was going to be a disaster, she sensed—a fencing match in words and actions, parrying thrusts and dodging the less than subtle attempts at seduction that Leo was bound to make. She was a fool to have agreed to it—and by the end of the evening she might be a sorry fool.

The silence lasted until they reached his cottage and he switched off the engine.

Then he turned to her, twisting sideways in the bucket seat of the little car, hitching up one leg so that his big knee thrust towards her. She wanted to touch it, to put her hand on it and feel its strength and warmth, but she didn't dare. That too made her angry—angry with herself, and even more afraid.

He regarded her steadily for a moment, then said, very quietly, 'Have I done something wrong?'

She didn't know how to answer, because in truth he had done very little apart from compliment her. It was her own weakness towards him that she resented. She shook her head. 'No—not really.'

'Will it help if I promise to behave like a gentleman?'

Abbie found herself laughing softly at the wry tone of his voice. 'Do you know how?'

His chuckle was self-deprecating. 'I might just be able to remember.'

She looked up and met his eyes, and although they were twinkling with humour they were also sincere. Suddenly she found she trusted him, and it was a novel sensation. She found herself wanting to explain her feelings, as much to herself as to him.

'You—you're pushing me,' she said slowly. 'I don't know how to deal with you, and you want to go so fast—I can't handle it. And yet,' she added honestly, 'there's a bit of me that wants to try.'

His hand came up and cupped the back of her neck, and slowly, gently, he pulled her towards him. 'Good,' he said softly, and his lips brushed hers in the lightest caress. He released her immediately, and she was shocked by the sudden sense of loss.

'Let's go and find something to eat.'

He hopped out over the door, and blindly, functioning very much on auto-pilot, she let herself out of the car and followed him into the house.

It was a typical Suffolk cottage, with low beams over the doorways and a massive inglenook dominating one end of the big kitchen. It was furnished in old pine, the walls white as befitted the beamed interior, but it lacked a woman's touch, Abbie thought. No plates on the walls or pretty chintz curtains, no bunches of dried herbs hanging over the heavy refectory table, no copper pans over the bressumer beam above the fireplace.

For some crazy reason that made her feel better, as if it indicated that no woman had paused here long enough to leave her mark on the place.

Not that she expected to, either. For another, and totally contradictory reason, that made her feel worse.

She sighed, and, shooting her a puzzled glance, Leo pulled out a carver chair at the head of the solid old refectory table and pushed her gently into it.

'You need a drink — dry white wine suit you?'

'Thank you.'

He set the glass down in front of her, the pale liquid gleaming in the sunlight that slanted through the window. It looked like a magic potion, she thought, and then wondered whose favour it would work in.

His, inevitably, as he had given it to her. She eyed it doubtfully.

'It isn't poisoned,' he told her, his voice candid, and she realised that once again he had read her thoughts.

'Can't I hide anything from you?' she asked him drily, and he chuckled.

'Sorry, I've been a doctor too long. I read minds as part of my professional qualifications.' He picked up her hand and held it loosely between his two. 'Abbie, relax,' he said. 'You're quite safe — even from yourself.'

He turned her hand over and pressed a kiss into the palm, sending her pulse rocketing and her mind into overdrive. Then he curled her fingers down over the kiss and laid her hand back gently on the table.

'I thought we'd have grilled trout and salad,' he said over his shoulder as he moved away from her, leaving her even more bewildered than before.

'Fine.' Her voice was strained, a little unsteady. Was this what it was like, to want someone so badly that you were unable to control your thoughts and actions? No wonder duels were fought and lovers were shot in their beds!

She sipped the wine cautiously, and found it cool and deliciously dry. She had a bigger sip, then set it down quickly before she could overdo it, content to watch Leo cooking.

More than content, in fact. His movements were swift, economical, precise — just like his surgery — and he hummed softly under his breath, clearly relaxed. Abbie wished she were more relaxed, but watching him — so close, so masculine, so damned desirable — did nothing for her relaxation.

She watched him anyway, the smooth ripple of corded muscle in his forearm as he sliced the ingredients for the salad, the way his trousers curved snugly over that neat, taut bottom when he crouched to check the fish —— She groaned softly and took another gulp of wine, closing her eyes. You could have too much of a good thing.

The trout was wonderful, moist and tender, cooked to perfection, the salad delicately dressed to blend perfectly with the subtle flavours. Abbie ate every scrap, finally pushing the empty plate away with a sigh of satisfaction.

'Wow.'

'Good?'

'Lovely — thank you.'

He cleared the plates into the sink and returned with a huge bowl of fresh raspberries picked that afternoon from his garden, and drowned in thick yellow cream.

'It's so bad for the heart,' she laughed, but he just smiled and picked up a raspberry and fed it to her with his fingers.

She took it with her teeth, unwilling to let her lips touch his fingers. It seemed too intimate, too ——

'My turn,' he said softly.

Heart pounding, she picked up a raspberry and held it out to him.

He had none of her inhibitions. He closed his teeth on the raspberry, and, grasping her hand, he drew each finger in turn into his mouth, wrapping his tongue around the tip and sucking gently, his eyes never leaving hers.

'Your turn again,' he said gruffly, and picked up one of the berries, dipping it deeply into the cream. 'Open.'

Her mouth opened of its own volition, and closed softly around his fingers. A tiny moan rose in her throat, and her lids drooped down over her eyes as she let her tongue explore the texture of his fingertips.

Then he withdrew them, and, cupping the back of her head, he drew her towards him and covered her lips with his.

They were soft, warm, tangy with the juice of the raspberries and oh, so gentle. She felt his tongue trace the outline of her lips, then the crease between them, coaxing them apart.

'Give me your mouth,' he murmured, and she surrendered to him, giving herself up absolutely to the sensations that rocked through her.

She made a small sound of protest when he lifted his head, but then she heard the scrape of the chair and he stood, pulling her to her feet and leading her through into the sitting-room.

Then he sat on the big armchair and drew her down on to his lap, tipping her sideways so that she lay cradled against his arm, his thighs firms against her bottom, the hard thrust of his arousal pressing against her hip as he slanted his lips over hers once more and thrust his tongue deeply into the soft recesses of her mouth.

She felt his fingers working the pins out of her hair, and then it was free and he was fanning it out, threading it through his fingers and murmuring softly, his words lost in their kiss.

She shifted against him and he growled low in his throat, then slipped one hand under her shirt and cupped a breast, rotating it under his palm as the nipple peaked and strained towards him. Lifting his head, he shifted so that he could see her, unbuttoning her shirt and gazing at her breasts with hooded eyes.

'Beautiful,' he muttered gruffly, and with deft fingers he slipped the catch and her breasts spilled out into his waiting hands. 'Oh, Abigail. . .'

Abbie watched, spellbound, as he lifted her breasts and buried his face between them. A low groan rumbled against her, and then she felt the chafe of his stubble on her skin as he turned his head and closed his mouth over one aching peak.

She clutched his head, threading her fingers through his hair and cradling him close, gasping as he bit gently on her nipple and then soothed it with little flicks of his tongue.

He turned his attention to the other one, his mouth hot against her skin, and she felt a shudder of need run through her.

He lifted his head and stared at her, his eyes glittering with the same need that she felt.

'Stop me, Abbie,' he muttered gruffly. 'For God's sake, stop me now.'

She stared at him numbly, too aroused to argue, too confused to reason with her senses.

After an age he sighed softly. 'Oh, damn you, Abigail, with your big innocent eyes,' he murmured, and his voice was ragged. He lowered his head again and kissed the smooth, creamy slope of her breasts before he refastened her bra and drew the edges of her blouse together. As he buttoned it, she noticed that his fingers were trembling, and she felt a quiver of shame and remorse. She should never have let things go so far——

'Don't,' he said harshly.

Her eyes flew up and met his; they were rich with understanding.

'If it's anybody's fault, it's mine. I promised to behave. You have nothing to be ashamed of or guilty about, Abigail. Do you hear me? Nothing.'

'I shouldn't have let it happen——'

'Hogwash. It was spontaneous and very beautiful. I just wish I hadn't had the pang of conscience that made me stop.'

His voice, though strained, was laced with humour, and Abbie saw tenderness blossom in his eyes. She reached up and cupped his cheek.

'I'm sorry I'm so old-fashioned. I expect your usual girlfriends know how to behave.'

His grin was wry. 'Don't you mean that they *don't* know how to behave? And anyway, what usual girl-friends? I don't have that many, Abbie.'

She laughed and wriggled off his lap, only too conscious that he was still aroused.

'Tell it to the fairies, Leo. I imagine you have to fend them off with a stick!'

'Only six days a week.'

'Don't tell me — on Sundays you give yourself a day off.'

He chuckled. 'Something like that.' He stood up, his body close to hers, and his hands came to rest on her shoulders, drawing her back against him. 'Don't run away from me, Abbie. Let me hold you for a moment.'

He turned her into his arms and her head found itself a little cradle in the hollow of his shoulder.

With a tiny sigh she settled against him, her arms around his waist, only too content to hold him close and let the ripples of need fade gradually away in the undemanding warmth of his embrace.

Tomorrow she would have to face him, to put their relationship back on to a professional footing. How she would do it she had no very clear idea, but she didn't intend to worry about it now.

Now she had more than enough to occupy her, with the warm, musky scent of his skin, the steady beat of his heart under her ear, the solid column of his spine beneath her hands.

She knew it was wrong to let herself stand like that in the circle of his arms, but somehow, just now, it seemed completely and unarguably right.

After an age he released her, and gave her a crooked little smile. 'I suppose I ought to take you home,' he said.

'Please.'

On the drive back her hair flew around and whipped in her eyes, and she gathered it up with one hand so that it didn't tangle. The other hand was trapped by Leo, pressed between his cool, dry palm and the firm muscle of his thigh.

She didn't even ask how he managed to change gear. She was too preoccupied with the subtle shift of muscle under her hand.

He drew up outside her flat and cut the engine, turning to her in the light from the street-lamps.

'Do you want me to see you in?'

She shook her head. 'I don't think that would be very wise. Thank you for a lovely evening, Leo.'

He held on to her hand. 'It doesn't have to end, you know.'

'It does,' she said softly.

'Spoilsport,' he said, very quietly, and then leaned forward and brushed his lips briefly with his. 'Go on, then. Wave from the window so I know you're all right.'

She slipped out of the car, let herself in and ran up the steps. He returned her wave, then pulled away, the soft burble of the exhaust the only sound in the still evening. She watched the lights fade, then paced aimlessly in the flat, only too conscious of the fact that she was alone — and she need not have been.

Abbie glanced up from the hated computer and found Leo lounging against the door-frame. Her last patient had just gone and she was hoping for a little tranquillity to sort out her disordered thoughts.

Instead she had Leo, the architect of her disorder. She groaned.

'Problems?'

'You're my worst problem,' she told him candidly, 'and just now I don't think I can cope with you.'

He shouldered himself away from the door-frame and sauntered over to the desk.

'Doctor, doctor, I think I'm a pack of cards. Sit over there and I'll deal with you later.'

She groaned again, and a crooked smile crinkled his lips.

'Now, how did I know you'd react like this?'

'Must be because you've been a doctor for so many years — or is it because of your dedicated study of body language?'

His grin widened. 'Let's just say you're pretty predictable, after a week and a half of the same reaction I'm getting to anticipate it.' He tapped some buttons on the computer, and the screen miraculously cleared, all tidied away.

What a shame she couldn't push buttons and tidy Leo away. Instead, Abbie thought with resignation, he was there beside her — *right* beside her! — and clearly not about to go away.

'Can I do something for you?' she asked, and then groaned inwardly at the teasing glint in his eye. 'Apart from that,' she added drily.

He chuckled. 'Yeah — another role-play exercise.'

'Oh, Leo, no, for God's sake —— !'

'Just a quickie. I'm a thirty-two-year-old professional

man and I've recently started suffering from insomnia. I come in and tell you I haven't been sleeping.'

'Any previous history I should know about?' she asked heavily.

'Nope. Fit as a flea.'

'Right, Mr Blank. How long has this been going on?'

'Oh, about ten days.'

She eyed him sceptically. 'Ten days?'

'Well, nights.'

'And can you think of any reason why you haven't been sleeping? Anything that you're worried about? Changes at work, redundancy threat—marriage difficulties?'

He sighed. 'No, no threats, and no marriage difficulties. I'm single, and currently I don't have a partner. There has been a change at work, though—a new member of staff.'

Abbie knew he was playing games, but she went along with him anyway—to an extent. 'Is he a threat?' she asked innocently.

'She—and no, not professionally. Mentally, though—and sexually—she's playing havoc with my life. You see, she's very lovely, sweet and innocent and very, very sexy, and every time I get into bed I imagine her there with me, those long, slender limbs wrapped around me, her sweet, soft mouth pressed against my skin, tasting me, crying out for me——'

Abbie pressed her hands against her flaming cheeks and shut her eyes tight to banish the images.

'Leo, for God's sake,' she whispered in a strangled voice.

'What is it, Abbie?' he murmured, his fingers trailing

hot circles against the back of her neck. 'You been having the same trouble sleeping?'

'No!' she protested weakly. 'Of course not. Why should I?'

'Because you feel the way I do—because you want me, too?'

'No,' she protested again, but it was a half-hearted protest because she was too honest to lie, and anyway, there was no point. He knew the simple truth, and the truth was that yes, she did want him. No, she had to try a different tack.

'We don't have to surrender to our instincts, Leo. That's what makes us different from animals.'

'But we don't have to be so busy proving that we aren't animals that we fail to enjoy one of the most exquisitely pleasurable aspects of being human,' he said softly.

She was struggling to resist the lure of his voice, ready to throw herself into his arms and to hell with common sense and propriety. 'What about freedom of choice?' she suggested as a last-ditch protest.

He grinned. 'I'm exercising it—I've chosen you.'

She gave an unladylike snort of laughter. 'Oh, God, Leo, I feel so privileged!'

'Sarky little madam,' he grumbled. 'Some people show no gratitude. Let me take you out for lunch.'

'No.'

'Why?'

'You know why!'

'I'm the duty doctor—I have to make a house call to a patient who just happens to live very close to this wonderful pub that does the most fantastic prawn salad sandwiches you have ever seen. I'll treat you.'

She sighed. 'How did you know that I love prawn sandwiches?'

'Intuition?'

'Hogwash.'

'That's my word.'

They laughed together, but then their eyes clashed and the laughter died, leaving a throbbing silence.

Abbie looked away first. 'Right—well, I'll get my things ready and freshen up—two minutes?'

'Fine. I'll see you in the car.'

He turned and walked out, and Abbie quelled the urge to watch him as he retreated down the corridor. Why couldn't she be turned on by his mind, or his compassionate nature, or his professional skill? she thought in disgust. Why did it have to be his sexy little bottom that left her weak at the knees? What was that American expression—cute buns? Too right, she thought, and sneaked a look just as he turned back.

'Are you coming?'

'Yes—of course.' She whipped her bag out of the drawer, slammed it shut and followed him down the corridor.

'Don't forget to go——'

'I'm going!' she bit out, and dived into the cloak-room. Trust a man never to let you live a thing down!

The patient, a Mrs Partridge, lived with her son in a large house out in the sticks, as Leo put it.

'Filthy rich but he's a total wimp—utterly undeserving. He won't make good use of his inheritance.'

Abbie thought he was being rather harsh and judge-mental, but then they arrived at the house and a man she took to be the son answered the door. She had to admit that he was, as Leo had said, a total wimp. Thin and straggly, he had pale skin and big, mournful eyes — eyes that kept following her, Abbie realised uncomfortably.

She was thankful when Leo shut him out of the room and introduced her to Mrs Partridge.

She was a large woman, with a capable air that belied her obvious frailty. She was propped against a mountain of cushions in the corner of a huge sofa, a long-haired cat curled up on her lap, and a box of liqueur chocolates open on the table beside her.

She offered them to Leo, and he took one and handed the box to Abbie.

'Thank you, no, I won't. I'm supposed to be on a diet ——'

'Good God, girl, whatever for?' Mrs Partridge exploded. 'You're lovely just as you are. Ridiculous nonsense!'

Abbie smiled and took a chocolate. 'Just one, then,' she conceded, and Leo winked and took the box from her, helping himself to another one.

'You'll be the death of me, Mrs P,' he mumbled round the chocolate, then perched on the footstool and took Mrs Partridge's once-capable hand in his. 'Now, what seems to be the matter this time?' Leo asked her.

'Damn all — stupid boy,' she said bluntly. 'Will insist on calling you out, Dr Chandler. I told him it was just a bit of dust in my eye, but he insisted I had conjuctivitis.'

Leo peered at her eyes. 'They look fine to me,' he told her.

'They are — perfectly all right. I found the speck of

dust and wiped it out with a handkerchief! I can't tell you how sorry I am.'

'Oh, well, since I'm here let's have a good look at you anyway,' he said with a grin, and she made a great production of unfastening her cardigan and sliding it off her shoulders to give him access to her arm.

He took her blood-pressure, sounded her chest, palpated her abdomen and then straightened. 'Well, you're no better and no worse than you were before. How are your ankles?'

'Fine — why? My heart about to pack up now, is it?'

Leo laughed. 'No, of course not. You've got a touch of congestion in your lungs, but nothing to worry about. Are you taking the tablets regularly?'

She snorted. 'He thinks so.'

'He?'

'Simon. He gives them to me every morning — I feed them to the plants. Doing well, they are.'

Leo shook his head. 'Really, Mrs P, you must take them. It's for your own good——'

'Oh, it's just a little game I play with him. He watches me, and I try to hide them. Pathetic, isn't it? Life's so damn boring I can't begin to tell you. If the only entertainment left is dicing with death, then I'll do it. God knows it can't be worse than being alive. The only thing that keeps me going is hoping that wet creature will get a little street-wise before I die, so he stands a chance of coping in the big wide world without my skirts to hide behind.'

She heaved a great sigh, and Leo patted her hand and pulled a sympathetic face. 'You never know, Marjorie, once you're gone he may find hidden strengths.'

She snorted expressively. 'Fat chance. They're too well-hidden for the idiot to find! Oh, well, not a thing I can do about it anyway, so I may as well not torture myself. Have another chocolate.'

Leo shook his head. 'No, thanks. Don't want to spoil my lunch.'

'Going to the Barley Mow for a prawn sandwich?'

He chuckled. 'Sly old thing, aren't you? Tell you the truth, I didn't really need to see you at all, I just used you as an excuse to get Abbie alone for a few minutes. Feed her well, I thought, and who knows?'

Her face softened with reminiscence. 'She'll like it there. Used to be our favourite haunt when Bill was alive. Ah, well. . . Give the place my love.'

'We will. Take care, now, and take the pills, please?'

'Bully,' she grumbled good-naturedly.

Leo opened the door and Simon all but fell through it.

'How is she, Doctor?' he asked worriedly.

'Fine—a speck of dust. Stop worrying about her; she's as strong as a horse.'

'She looks frail sometimes.'

'She is frail sometimes—she's old. But she's not stupid, and she's not in any immediate danger, so try not to worry.'

They made their escape and Leo phoned in and checked with the surgery before heading for the pub.

'No more calls?' Abbie said in disbelief.

'None that wants to see me. I'm too ruthless.'

'Oh, yeah, I've just seen how ruthless you are— stuffing liqueur chocs and nattering about pubs and prawn sandwiches——'

'Ah, well, Marjorie's special.'

'Leo, they're all special to you. How's little Maxie Clarke with her glandular fever?'

'OK — not co-operating very well, but then she never does.'

'How about Mary Tanner?'

'Ah, Mary — I wonder when Gerry will come in? I'd like you in on that consultation. Terminal care is one of my pet areas, and I'd like to deal with it myself, but on the other hand I think you could learn a lot. I'll check with them and see if we can work alongside.'

Abbie felt doubtful, and said so. 'I'm not sure I've got anything to offer,' she said quietly. 'All that emotion — it's a bit daunting.'

'You soon get used to sorting through the different vibes and working out what the real problem is. Wait and see. You might change your mind.'

They turned into the pub car park and Leo pulled up under a leafy weeping willow tree. The branches trailed down around them, almost completely enclosing them in a pale green cocoon.

'Have I told you today how very lovely you are?' he asked softly.

She felt her cheeks heat, and looked away.

'Come on, no false modesty; you're beautiful.'

'And you're a smooth-talking con man,' she told him bluntly.

'No, I'm not. Come here, I want to kiss you.'

'Take a hike.'

'No.'

He reached across and put a single finger under her chin, exerting almost no force.

It must have been the magic of the willow tree, or a trick of the light, or a will-o'-the-wisp. Whatever, her head turned, angling towards him, and as his lips came down and fused with hers in the soft green shade she surrendered more than her lips to him.

She surrendered her soul.

CHAPTER FIVE

GERRY TANNER came to see Leo on Friday afternoon, the last appointment of the day. Leo called Abbie in, having consulted with Gerry, and she found herself a seat out of the way and settled down to watch Leo in action.

Gerry started off by discussing Mary's treatment, and it was obvious from the way he was talking that he refused to accept the inevitability of her death.

'This radiotherapy,' he said, 'how many courses will she need to knock this bone thing on the head — or won't it?'

Leo hesitated, letting the silence speak for a moment, then sighed softly. 'The radiotherapy will relieve her pain, and knock out isolated tumours which are pressing on nerves and causing referred pain. It won't make the problem go away.'

'So what will?'

Again Leo paused, but Gerry jumped in again.

'More chemotherapy? Perhaps she didn't have enough. A bone marrow transplant? Maybe I should take her to Switzerland to one of these clinics ——' He ground to a halt, clearly realising the futility of his train of thought.

Leo let the silence continue, and finally Gerry lifted his head. His eyes were bleak.

'There must be something we can do.'

79

Leo reached out a hand and laid it on Gerry's knee. 'I'm sorry.'

'I could take her to Lourdes.'

'You could—if you really felt it would do any good—or you could spend time with her, talking to her, helping each other to understand and supporting each other, not wasting the precious time you have left.'

Gerry sat in silence, absorbing Leo's words, and then he gave a short grunt of laughter. 'She said that, the other day. She got mad with me because she wanted to go out and I was fiddling about doing something not really necessary. "For God's sake stop wasting time!" she said, and I thought she was just having a go at me, but she wasn't, was she? She was saying she didn't have time to waste. . .'

He dropped his head into his hands, and a harsh sob tore out of his chest. He slumped across the desk, buried his face in his arms and wept as if his heart was breaking—which of course it was.

Leo laid a large, comforting hand on Gerry's head and smoothed his hair back, as one would with a distressed child. 'How about rustling up some tea, Abbie?' he said quietly, and she nodded and slipped out, only too glad to get away from all that raw emotion.

When she went back in Gerry was sitting up again, back in control once more but still clearly very upset.

'The cavalry,' Leo said with a slight smile, and she put the tray down on the desk and handed each of them a cup.

Gerry took it and gave a weary smile. 'Thanks. Sorry about that. I've been avoiding the truth for so long. . .'

He swore softly, then apologised. 'It just hurts so bloody much.'

'It will,' Leo told him. 'Look at it this way—if it didn't hurt, she wouldn't be worth knowing. There's a saying—the bit that hurts is the bit that cares. That's very true, you know.'

Gerry nodded, deep in thought, then shot Leo a hesitant look. 'Talking of hurting, Mary asked me to make love to her the other night, but I couldn't. I made some excuse about being too tired, but really I was just scared to death of hurting her. I mean—can I? Will it hurt?'

Leo shrugged thoughtfully. 'Don't know. It shouldn't at the moment, if she hasn't got any pelvic or hip involvement, but she can always tell you. Damn it, you've got brakes, Gerry. You can easily stop if it does.'

He nodded. 'Yeah—I suppose so.' He swallowed. 'I don't know if I can—well—bring myself to do it. Somehow it seems wrong to do something so—I dunno—when she's dying.'

'Something so what?' Leo asked gently. 'So loving? So sharing? So giving?'

Gerry and Leo stared at each other for a moment, then Gerry's mouth lifted in a sad little smile. 'We always had a good sex-life—for both of us. We were well-matched, I suppose. Recently, though. . .' He shrugged. 'It just hasn't happened. I still love her, though. . .' His voice cracked again, and he put the cup down abruptly and dragged in a deep breath. 'Sorry.'

'Don't worry about it. Try again, Gerry. Get someone to have the kids for the night and spoil yourselves.'

He nodded. 'Yes, I suppose we could. Seems a bit premeditated, though.'

Leo grinned. 'All adds to the anticipation.'

Gerry chuckled. 'I guess so. I'm just afraid — all that emotion — I'll make a fool of myself.'

'By crying with her? I should think it's inevitable, but it'll get you closer, and get you talking again. She needs you, Gerry — she needs you a great deal. You have so much to give her at this time.'

He swallowed and nodded, then, draining his tea, he stood up and held out a hand to Leo.

'Sorry it all got so undignified, but I feel a lot better now — clearer, somehow. Thanks,' he said sheepishly, and Leo slung an arm round his shoulder and gave him a quick hug of comfort.

'Any time. You've got my home number, haven't you? Ring if you need me.'

'Thanks, I will.'

He left, looking better than when he had come in, and Abbie watched him go.

'Poor man.'

'At least he's making progress now.'

'Mmm.'

'What are you doing tomorrow?'

She turned to him with a tired smile. 'Studying?'

'Wrong.'

She groaned. 'No, Leo, not role play!'

He chuckled. 'No way. No, let's go and play on the river.'

'What?'

'We can go up to the Broads and go for a row, and pick up a pub lunch.'

Abbie hesitated.

'It'll be cooler on the water,' he coaxed softly, and she was lost.

'What time?' she sighed.

His grin was victorious. 'Ten—and wear something casual.'

It was another radiantly beautiful day, the sun suspended in a sky of Mediterranean blue, and Abbie smothered her face in sun-screen and twisted her hair up under a large floppy straw hat. She was wearing light cotton trousers and a baggy T-shirt with elbow-length sleeves to protect her skin from the sun, and she put a pair of old tennis shoes on her bare feet.

Leo arrived promptly at ten, and she was relieved to see he was similarly dressed—except that he wore shorts. Not cut-offs or anything too outrageous, just tailored, fairly long shorts that even so showed off his straight, firmly muscled and hair-scattered legs to perfection.

'All set?' he asked, and she nodded, trying not to stare. 'Right, let's go.'

She followed him down the stairs, locking the door behind them and following him to the car parked a little further up the road.

'I've brought Topsy again—thought we could do with the air-conditioning,' he told her with a grin.

Abbie chuckled. 'You're crazy.'

'I try to be—only way to stay sane,' he said, and hopped over the door, sliding his long legs under the wheel.

Abbie climbed in the more conventional way, relieved to have trousers on so that she didn't have to battle with the riding hemline syndrome.

It was a lovely drive, and, with one hand clamped firmly to the top of her head to anchor the hat, Abbie turned her face up to the sun and leant back on the head-rest, sighing with contentment.

Life was good, she mused. OK, general practice was a bit of a rat at the moment, but maybe it would get better. Meanwhile there was sunshine, and she had the weekend off—and so did Leo.

Her heart did a little tango, and she slid a glance across at him. He was lightly tanned, his skin glowing with health, and as she watched he flicked a glance in her direction and his mouth curled in a lazy, sexy smile.

'OK?' he asked, and she nodded.

'Fine?'

'Good.' His hand came out and found her fingers, threading through them, and he rested the back of her hand on his thigh just below the cuff of his shorts.

She could feel the rough hairs against her skin, and the warmth of his thigh where the sun had been on it, and she had an almost overwhelming urge to turn her hand over and run it slowly over his leg, testing the texture with her fingertips, the rough hair over satin skin, and the hard ridges of muscle beneath, shifting when he changed gear, sending quivers up her spine.

It was almost a relief when he pulled up outside a stretch of water, turned the car into a little car-park and switched off the engine.

'We're here,' he said unnecessarily, and she picked up her few things and climbed out.

He snapped the tonneau cover on over the cockpit, pocketed the keys and went and paid the car-park attendant.

'Right, let's find a boat,' he said with a grin, and,

draping an arm casually over her shoulders, he steered
her over the road and down to a little jetty.

He paid the boatman and jumped down into the
boat, turning to help Abbie in. Water, she had to
acknowledge, was not her most natural medium, but
even so she managed not to make too big a fist of
climbing into the boat.

'Right, sit there,' Leo instructed, and after position-
ing her in the stern he sat in the midsection of the boat,
placed his legs each side of hers and picked up the
oars.

'I suppose you can row?' she said mildly.

He snorted, and with a deft twist of the wrist he
slotted the oars into the rowlocks and pushed off.

In moments they were cruising peacefully along away
from the crowds, and Abbie was able to settle back in
the stern and watch him.

'I think you're enjoying watching me do all the
work,' he said after a while.

Abbie, who was enjoying it enormously, agreed with
a smile. 'You do it so well,' she said.

'Humph. You can have a go, you know — you only
have to say the word.'

'Later.' She settled back with a sigh and turned her
face to the sun. 'Bliss.'

Cold water splashed across her, and she opened her
eyes to find Leo watching her, a slow smile playing
across his face. 'Sorry,' he said unrepentantly.

'I'll bet. Is it my turn or something?'

'Want to try?'

'Only if you can cope with my lack of aptitude.'

He chuckled. 'I'll tough it out. Come on, then,
change places, but do it slowly.'

They slid to opposite sides of the little boat, then Leo helped her on to the centre bench and shifted across into the stern.

That safely accomplished, he then took her little hands in his, put them on the oars and showed her the action.

'OK?'

She nodded dubiously, and so he let her go. Seconds later he was drenched.

'In the water, not across the top!' he yelled, and, grabbing her hands, he demonstrated again.

Again she soaked him, helpless with laughter by now, and he was forced to grab the oars and steer them round another boat.

'Idiot woman,' he chided laughingly. 'Now, come on, concentrate — not like that!'

He ducked, the boat hit a log under the water and wobbled wildly, and Abbie folded up on the bench, tears of laughter streaming down her cheeks.

'Useless — typical woman. Come on, let me do it.'

He stood up — but so did Abbie. The boat rocked wildly, Leo flapped his arms and with a wild yell sailed cleanly over the side.

Seconds later he came up, water streaming off him, and hauled himself over the side, waterweeds and all.

Abbie didn't know whether to laugh or run.

'Nice swim?' she asked him, and then a wicked little giggle forced its way out and escaped. She should have run.

The water wasn't as cold as she expected, she thought as she surfaced seconds later.

Leo was sitting in the boat regarding her impassively. She swam to the side.

'That was a despicable trick!' she told him as severely as she could manage.

'Mmm. Are you going to behave now, or do I leave you there?'

'Behave?' she spluttered. 'What have *I* done wrong?'

'Laughed at me. I could get petty about that.'

She grabbed a handful of weed and hurled it at him. 'I'll give you petty ——'

'Uh-uh!' he warned. 'You want to come back in the boat, you have to behave. Now, which is it to be?'

'I'll behave — give me a hand up.'

He leant over and hauled her up into the boat, depositing her on the stern.

'Now sit there, and for God's sake don't move!' he ordered.

'Aye-aye, Cap'n,' she said.

He snorted, and eyed her thoughtfully for a moment. 'That waterweed suits you,' he said eventually. 'You should wear it in your hair more often. Have you got a change of clothes with you?'

'Of course not — have you?'

'No.'

'Hmm.'

'We'd better go home.'

'Yes, we had.'

They looked at each other for a moment, then a slow smile crept over his face. 'You're wet,' he said softly.

'Oh, very acute ——'

'It has its advantages. . .'

Abbie glanced down, and saw with horror that her T-shirt was plastered against her body — her cold body. Her nipples were predictably at attention, and clearly visible. She tugged the T-shirt away from them and folded her arms defensively across her chest.

'Spoilsport,' he murmured.

'Just row,' she told him, and with a mock-salute he picked up the oars and headed back to the landing stage.

'Minor mishap,' he told the worried boatman, and Abbie followed him out of the boat and across the road, her shoes squelching with every step.

'I feel a right pillock,' she told him bluntly when they reached the car.

He turned and ran his eyes thoughtfully over her body. 'You look a right pillock,' he said.

'Thanks.'

'My pleasure. Are you going to take any of that lot off, or are you going to ruin my upholstery?'

'Take it off?' she squawked. 'In a crowded car park on a Saturday in August? Leave it out, Chandler! And what do you mean, ruin?' she added contemptuously.

'Back to that again, are we?' He sighed. 'Oh, well, it was just an idea.'

'It was a lousy one. What are you taking off?'

'Me?' He looked surprised. 'Nothing.'

'Fine.' She opened the door, plopped wetly on to the seat and stared straight ahead.

He joined her seconds later, fired up the car and headed for home.

It was a cold, miserable journey. Halfway there he stopped to put up the hood, which at least kept the draughts out a little, and he put the heater on too, but nevertheless Abbie was still frozen by the time they reached his cottage.

'What are we doing here?' she asked him tautly. 'I need to go home.'

'Like that, in the middle of a busy shopping day? I don't think it would do your reputation any good.'

'Well, whose fault is that?' she snapped, too cold and fed up to care about offending him. 'May I remind you that I wasn't the one who fell in? I was quite dry until you decided to have your fun!'

'So let me make amends,' he said quietly. 'Hot shower, then borrow one of my T-shirts and a pair of shorts and lie in the garden while the washing machine deals with your clothes. Then later on after we've had a meal somewhere I can take you back, all respectable again, and nobody will be any the wiser.'

It sounded tempting. For one thing she didn't fancy sitting in her soggy clothes another minute, and for another she knew there would be no hot water in her flat for a least an hour after she got home, and the thought of a shower was too wonderful for words.

She opened the door and peeled herself away from the seat, carrying her sodden shoes in her hand. She couldn't bear the thought of putting them back on.

He opened the door and led her in, showing her to the downstairs shower-room off the kitchen.

'You use this one and I'll go upstairs — unless you'd rather have a bath?'

She shook her head. 'No, thanks, I've been wallowing in this river water for quite long enough. I want to wash it off, not dilute it.'

He chuckled. 'Fine. I'll see you in a minute.'

She went into the shower-room, and, shutting the door gratefully behind her, she turned on the shower tap and held out her hand under the stinging spray. In seconds the water was piping hot, and she quickly stripped off her clothes and was about to step into the shower when she realised there was no towel.

She opened the door a little way to call for Leo, and froze.

He was standing in the utility-room, his soggy clothes in one hand, and, from his straight, hairy toes upwards over his lean, honed, well-muscled body, he was stark naked. She snapped her eyes up to his face, her breath clogged in her throat, hot colour burning her cheeks.

'Did you want something?' he asked calmly.

'A—a towel,' she mumbled. 'Sorry, I didn't realise you were—there. . .'

She dragged the door shut and hauled in a lungful of air. Dear God, why had the sight of him affected her so much? She was used to naked men—heavens, her brothers had hardly made a secret of their anatomy while they were growing up, and in the course of her work she was constantly confronted by nakedness in part if not in total.

So why had the sight of Leo's body made her feel as if her chest had been run over by a steamroller?

She dragged in another lungful of air, and then jumped when there was a tap on the door.

'Abbie? I've brought you a towel,' he said, and the door opened behind her back.

Unable to help herself, she turned, mesmerised, and looked up at him.

His eyes locked with hers, the blue more brilliant than ever, the gold like tiny sparks, glittering with need. For an age they stood frozen, face to face, unable to look away or hide from the truth.

Abbie's heart raced against her ribs, her blood roaring in her ears, the heat pooling low down in her aching body. Desire, fierce, primitive and unrelenting, tore through her, destroying her defences at a stroke.

Leo moved at last, his hand coming up to brush her cheek, his fingertips straying over her throat in the lightest of caresses. They paused, hovering over the pulse that hammered there, reading her reaction to his touch.

Her own hand lifted, resting lightly over his heart, feeling the pounding beat against her palm.

'Abbie?' he asked softly, and her lids fluttered closed, unable to resist the message in his eyes.

How could she, when she needed him so badly?

She knew it was wrong, stupid, hasty, that she would regret it later, but for now, this minute, this second, it was the right thing to do.

He reached past her and adjusted the shower, then pushed her gently towards it, following her in and twitching the curtain shut behind him.

His hands plucked the soap from the dish and then firmly, and without any attempt at seduction, he washed her all over, his hands thorough and business-like, but stopping at nothing.

By the time he had finished she was trembling from head to toe.

He handed her the soap. 'Your turn.'

She closed her eyes, hardly able to bear the pro-tracted intimacy that would be involved. She needed him — needed him now, needed to feel his weight on her, his body locked with hers, bringing an end to this terrible thing that was ruling her so fiercely.

How could he remain so totally unmoved? she

wondered, and then, as her hands travelled over him bit by bit, she realised that he was far from unmoved. His breathing was shallow and ragged, he was trembling all over, and he was quite clearly aroused.

Unmoved? she thought as she stood in front of him and smoothed her soapy hands down his back. Oh, no. Anything but. Her hands slid down, slick with soap, and curved over his buttocks, firm and taut, clenching under her hands, then round over the hollow by his hips, then on, dragging a shuddering groan from his throat.

'Enough, Abbie, for God's sake,' he choked out, and, reaching behind her, he cut the water off and stepped out. 'Here.'

He handed her a towel and then picked up the other, rubbing himself briskly all over before wrapping it round his hips.

She dried her trembling body self-consciously, unsure what the next move was. The protocol of lovemaking was something she had never had to trouble herself with, her only experience having been messy, unbelievably painful and a great many years before.

She knew enough now to know that the fumblings of her brother's friend had been crude and untutored in the extreme. However, that didn't help her now, and she stood, head bent, waiting for Leo to make the next move. Please, God, let it be soon.

She felt his finger under her chin, tipping her face up towards him, and she met his eyes hesitantly.

'Abbie? Is something wrong?'

She shook her head. 'No — it's just — I haven't done this for a while.'

'Do you want me to use a condom?'

Oh, God, she hadn't even thought that far. Her eyes fluttered shut. 'Please,' she mumbled.

'Come on.' He took her hand in his and led her out of the shower-room, across the kitchen and up the stairs to his bedroom at the end of the landing. Once there he pushed her down on to the edge of the bed and took a hairdryer out of a drawer.

Then, slowly and methodically, he dried her hair and teased out the tangles until it was smooth and dry and gleaming.

'Beautiful,' he murmured softly, and, putting down the hairdrier, he drew her to her feet and removed her towel, leaving her naked.

'I want you, Abbie,' he said gruffly. 'I need you.'

Then, lifting her in his arms, he laid her in the centre of the bed and came down beside her, his face just inches from hers, their bodies aligned from shoulder to toe.

Abbie ached for him, her body trembling with suspense and quivering on the verge of sanity.

'Leo, please,' she whispered, but he wasn't ready yet. He let his hands trail slowly over her, taking her to fever pitch, his lips following with a devastating intimacy that left Abbie shaken and beyond words.

Then, when she could bear it no longer, he moved over her, his body shaking under her hands, and claimed her with one long, steady stroke that shattered the last shreds of her control.

She buried her face in his shoulder and clung to him while the sensations dragged her down like a whirlpool, leaving her helpless in his arms.

'OK?' he asked softly.

Words escaped her. Eyes closed, still shaken by her reaction, she nodded slightly. His lips brushed her eyelids, then moved down, his mouth gentle against hers, undemanding for now. He let her rest for a moment, then slowly, carefully, he began to move again.

Abbie thought she had reached the limits of physical sensation. She was wrong. Leo drove her up again, relentless, his body demanding her response, and, like a flower opening in the sun, she gave him his reward.

This time when the end came he was with her, his body shuddering, racked with great tremors that echoed Abbie's own, and then he collapsed against her, his weight so welcome, completing her.

Abbie fell asleep instantly.

She woke before Leo. He had rolled on to his back and now lay spread-eagled across the bed, his big body totally relaxed, his chest rising and falling evenly.

Sitting up, her arms wrapped round her updrawn knees, she studied him while he slept, noting the pattern of hair that curled in soft profusion over his chest, arrowing down over the flat, smooth planes of his abdomen to widen again, making a cradle for his masculinity.

His body looked so innocent now, slaked and passionless — almost impossible to believe that it could do such incredible things to her.

She flushed, remembering her reaction, and looked away. Had she really behaved like that? Allowed him such intimacy? Such undreamt-of access to her inner-most secrets?

She moaned softly. How could she face him? What

should she say? Wow, big fella, that was the most amazing episode of my entire life? Or should she just ignore it, pretend that it was commonplace, an ordinary event?

For all she knew it might have been! How could she possibly tell? Maybe that was how it always was.

She heard him stirring, then felt a touch against her shoulder, light as a cobweb in a breeze.

'Abbie?' His voice was gruff with sleep, warm and deep. She felt her body quicken again. How did he do that to her? She felt terribly naked and vulnerable, and wished they were under the quilt. She hugged her knees tighter.

'Are you OK? Did I hurt you?'

She shook her head. Words still refused to come, locked in her throat.

'Come here. . .'

His hand cupped her shoulder, easing her down against him, and his lips found hers, soft and warm, filled with tenderness. She shivered, and he knelt up and lifted her against his chest, working the quilt down and snuggling them both beneath it.

'Better?'

She nodded.

'You must have got chilled in the river. Do you want a drink?'

She shook her head, still unable to look him in the eye. Every time she remembered her reaction, she felt crippled with shyness. Usually a very private person, she found displays of emotion very unsettling— especially her own.

Leo, on the other hand, had been displaying his

emotions for her very clearly since the day they had met.

'What's wrong?' he asked softly.

'Nothing,' she managed, but he wasn't fooled. He tipped her chin up and forced her to look at him.

'Liar,' he murmured. 'You're ashamed, aren't you? Ashamed of your reaction, ashamed of your weakness, ashamed of your beautiful body and its incredible responses. Oh, Abbie, what a waste.'

She flushed and looked away. 'It's easy for you.'

'Why? Because I don't think there's anything wrong with two people finding pleasure in each other's body?'

'There should be a relationship——'

'We have a relationship.'

'No, we don't. We work together.'

He laughed softly. 'Abbie, I've never felt the urge to make love to Colin or Peter or Ravi.'

She blushed furiously but he wouldn't give up.

'Come on, just admit it—we're good together, Abbie. That wasn't ordinary, was it? Something special happened there, something rare and beautiful. Don't be ashamed of it, please. It demeans it, nullifies it, makes it cheap. Don't do that to us, please. It may not be happy ever after, but it's no less valid.'

Abbie took a shaky breath and made herself meet his eyes. 'It just—caught me by surprise. I don't—I didn't realise. . .'

His hand cupped her cheek, his palm warm and dry, slightly rough. 'Trust me,' he said softly, then his lips came down and brushed hers once, twice. 'I want to make love to you again, Abigail.'

She swallowed, her eyes trapped by his.

'Let me touch you, love you. Let me show you what you body can do.'

Desire stabbed through her, leaving her limbs heavy and her heart pounding.

'Yes,' she murmured.

CHAPTER SIX

MONDAY — and reality — came all too soon. The week-end had passed in a blur of sensation, and after Leo had returned her to her flat on Sunday night she had fallen straight into bed and slept through to the morning without stirring.

Now, with surgery looming and the practice meeting to start the whole week off, she left her car in the car park and made her way slowly up the steps and into the office.

Ravi and Peter were there already with Peggy, and as she greeted everyone and sat down Leo arrived.

She couldn't look at him, convinced that all the most intimate details of their weekend were branded on her forehead in letters a foot high.

He dropped into the chair beside her, slid his foot up against hers and winked.

'Hi.'

'Good morning,' she said, very formally, and quietly prayed for him to behave. Fat chance.

'You look beautiful.'

'Leo, shut up,' she hissed.

He chuckled, and reached for the coffee Peggy pushed automatically towards him.

'Right, what's on the agenda?'

Abbie couldn't afterwards have told anyone what had taken place at the meeting. The entire time she had been conscious of nothing but Leo and his leg, sliding sensuously against hers, the heat of his skin burning her through the fine cotton of his trousers.

She moved her leg away several times but his followed it, hooked round it and brought it back every time.

In the end she decided it would be less conspicuous if she left it where it was, but the effect on her concentration was disastrous. She was only too relieved when the meeting ground to a halt and she could escape to her surgery.

The week improved at that point, because her first patient was Lorraine Creasey, the young woman with the query malignant melanoma that Leo had excised the previous week. The histology report showed no malignant changes, and so after checking that the wound was healing nicely Abbie was able to send her on her way greatly relieved.

The week then took a downturn. Her third patient that morning was Simon Partridge, the son of the woman with the liqueur chocolates—near the prawn sandwiches pub with the willow tree under which Leo had kissed her.

Abbie was less than thrilled to see him, even more so when it became obvious that there was little wrong with him. Either that, or she was an even worse doctor than she thought she was.

'I really can't see anything wrong with your throat, Mr Partridge,' she told him, 'but, just to reassure us both, I'll take a swab and get it sent off. You should be able to ring in for the result at the end of the week.'

'Thank you so much,' he said, with what Abbie thought was undue sincerity. She slipped the swab into the tube, sealed it and labelled it and asked after his mother as she did so.

'Oh, well, I think she's all right at the moment — I worry about her.'

'I don't think you need to — she seems really very well for her age,' Abbie assured him. He opened his mouth and she sensed a long dissertation on his mother's state of health, and leapt in hastily. 'Not that she's my patient, you understand, and any discussion about her really should be conducted with Dr Chandler. Right, goodbye, Mr Partridge — don't forget to phone at the end of the week.'

He stood up, thanked her again and then reached over the desk and held out his hand, leaving her no polite alternative but to shake it.

Not a pleasant experience. It was cool, slightly damp and curiously insistent. She pulled hers away as soon as courtesy allowed, and pressed the buzzer for the next patient, thus giving him no option but to leave.

He did so, clearly reluctantly, and left Abbie feeling puzzled and not a little uncomfortable. Had he come to see her because there was something other than his throat wrong and she'd cut him off before he had time to air his fears?

Either that or, much more unpalatable, he had come on the pretext of his throat just to see her.

Her fertile imagination leapt ahead, imagining all sorts of ghastly scenarios, and she reined herself in sharply and gave her attention to her next patient.

Leo came in with a cup of coffee for her just after her last patient left, and perched on the corner of her desk. 'Busy morning?'

'Mmm. Thanks for the coffee.' She avoided his eye.

'You're welcome — think of it as a peace offering for playing footsie during the meeting.'

She shot him a black look. 'Hmm. You weren't exactly subtle.'

His mouth tipped into a heart-stopping smile. 'Abbie?'

Damn, that voice like liquid chocolate slithered over her senses, turning her to mush.

'What?'

'Look at me.'

She forced herself to meet his eyes.

'You're beautiful.' His hand reached out and smoothed her cheek. 'I'm sorry if I wore you out — did you sleep well?'

Her cheek warmed beneath his palm. 'Like a log,' she mumbled, and her eyes slid away.

Even now, after all that had happened between them, she still found it hard to look at him.

Leo tipped her head round towards him again. 'Don't hide from me, Abbie, or try and pretend nothing's happened,' he growled softly, and there was a steely glint in his eye.

She turned her head away again. 'I'm not, Leo — it's just that I haven't had any practice at this sort of thing, and I'm confused. It all happened so fast — I need time to adjust — to sort out my feelings.'

'What's to sort out? We're adults, Abbie. We went to bed.'

She looked at him then. 'Is that all?' she asked softly, and this time it was he who looked away.

'Sure — what else? Damn it, Abbie, what do you want? A declaration of undying love?'

She was a little shocked to find that she did. She denied it, though, still trying to assimilate the implications.

'Of course not — it would hardly be realistic so soon, but — just sex?'

He shrugged. 'What's wrong with that?'

'Nothing — if it was the truth, but I don't think it was.'

He gave a sharp sigh. 'Don't get all hearts and flowers on me, Abbie,' he growled.

'I like that! It was you who told me it was something special!' she retorted crossly. 'I've said I don't expect a declaration of love ——'

'But I get the distinct impression you wouldn't mind.'

'I would — if it were a lie.'

'I wouldn't lie to you, Abbie. Yes, it was great — there's something incredible that happens between us when we touch — but it's still just physical. Don't lie to yourself, Abigail. There's nothing wrong with sex — nothing at all.'

Abbie said nothing, and after a moment Leo stood up. 'I have to go and see Maxie again — she's not making any progress, and it's been a fortnight. I think I'll try and get some blood from her. Want to witness a riot?'

He was all professional doctor again, the lover set aside — although not, Abbie was sure, for long.

'Yes, I'll come. What time?'

'When you're ready. Oh, what did Simon Partridge want?'

She gave a hollow laugh. 'Search me. He said he had a sore throat, but I couldn't see anything. I took a swab, but I got the funniest feeling about him.'

'Mmm. Watch him; he's a bit odd about women.'

'Odd? You mean gay?'

Leo laughed abruptly. 'Lord, no. Rather the opposite—and don't worry, he hasn't been done for rape or indecent exposure or anything, he just tends to get a bit fixated. They had a groom at the stable there once who left because he wouldn't take the hint and leave her alone. His mother was hysterically funny on the subject.'

'I wonder if she isn't the cause of half his problems?'

Leo chuckled. 'Undoubtedly, I should have thought. Oh, what was the histology on Lorraine Creasey?'

'Clear—she was delighted.'

'Good. How does it look?'

'Hardly a mark—should heal very well. Clever old you.'

'Wow—praise for something at last!'

'You got plenty of praise at the weekend,' she said without thinking, and then could have bitten her tongue off.

Leo chuckled. 'So I did—fancy me forgetting a thing like that. Come on, let's go and see Maxie and then pay Colin a visit—it's time he came back and took over your training.'

Abbie blinked. She had forgotten that Colin Williams, the senior partner, was supposed to be dealing with her training, and that Leo was only standing in for him.

'You in a hurry to hand me back?' she asked.

He tipped a finger under her chin and winked. 'Nope. Just thought you might learn more if your trainer wasn't being constantly distracted by your delectable body.'

She flushed and dropped her lashes. 'Leo. . .'

'Ah, well, I dare say if you sat on the other side of a screen we might be able to do a better job.'

'You just have no self-control,' she chided him.

'Look who's talking.'

She blushed again. He was right; she had none where he was concerned — well, not any more. She had hung on for a while — a very short while. It was, after all, only three weeks since she had started at the practice and two weeks since Leo had come back from his holiday.

Two short weeks, in which she had fallen headlong for the man and granted him liberties which even now made her blush ——

'Penny for them.'

'Not on your life,' she muttered, and, grabbing her bag, she followed him out.

Maxie was, as he'd said, little better. She was listless and floppy, her throat was still sore, and the chain of glands running down the sides of her neck were clearly visible. There was no doubt now that she had glandular fever, and so Leo was quite happy to abandon the blood test with all its traumatic implications and pre-scribe rest, plenty of fluids and more rest.

Maxie, however, was bored with resting and although she had no energy she still insisted on getting up very early and playing the piano for four hours every morning.

'Thank goodness it's the school holidays or she'd probably insist on going there, too!' her exhausted mother told them.

'It's the need to repeat things, to set up obsessive

patterns and follow them doggedly come what may, that's so wearing,' Leo elaborated after they had left.

'Her mother looks shattered,' Abbie agreed. 'Does she get any relief? Anyone to share the burden of care?'

Leo shook his head. 'Well, her husband comes back home from Norwich every evening, and usually he brings work home at the weekend as well, I gather.'

'So not a lot of support there.'

'You could say that. I think the whole thing's a bit much for him. They split up some time ago, but he came back after a few months. I think they live essentially separate lives, though.'

'Poor woman — it's a lot to cope with on your own.'

'The chains of love — if you don't have a family, you can't get lumbered.'

'And what a boring and unfulfilling life it would be!'

Leo gave a grunt of laughter. 'You reckon? I think you'd find Maxie's mother might disagree, and her father certainly would.'

Abbie fell silent, not convinced that Leo was right. Her own family was very close, and although they were, to a certain extent, dependent on each other they also supported each other through difficult times and periods of change. In a way their dependence gave them freedom, because they had the security of their family's love behind them.

Had Leo's family life been unhappy? He hadn't mentioned any relatives — although, she had to admit, neither had she. They hadn't spent their time together talking, in the main.

'You're looking thoughtful.'

She glanced across at him. 'I was just wondering

about your family—realising, I suppose, that I know nothing, but nothing, about you.'

His mouth quirked into a smile. 'Oh, yeah? I would have said you knew a great deal about me.'

She blushed and looked down at her hands. 'I may know a lot about one small aspect of you——'

'Are you being insulting?' he asked wickedly, and she laughed, unable to help herself.

'Of your personality, then. But I don't know if your parents are still alive, if you have brothers and sisters, where they all live, how you got on with them when you were growing up—any of it.'

'Is this a "What are your prospects, son?" conversation?' he asked drily.

'It's your past, not your future that I'm asking about,' she told him, just as drily.

'Silly me. Right, let's see what I can tell you. I'm an only child, my parents are both still practising GPs in Oxfordshire, very much alive and pillars of the local community—Mum's a counsellor for Relate, Dad's a JP. I went to boarding-school in Norfolk at the age of eight, then to Barts for my medical training. I'm thirty-two, six feet two tall, I weigh about thirteen stone, like grotty old cars and fast women.'

'Humph!'

'Is that all? I give you my life story and you say, "Humph"!'

She laughed softly. 'I humphed about the fast women.'

'Don't you believe it?'

She swivelled in her seat and eyed him thoughtfully. 'I did,' she said slowly, 'but I'm not so sure I do any more. I think it's just a front.'

'A front?' He laughed, she thought a little self-consciously. 'A front for what, for God's sake?'

'Your shy, retiring, stay-at-home side, the side that likes to lie in the garden and listen to the bees, or go rowing on the river, or curl up in front of sentimental old movies——'

'You're nuts! Sentimental old movies?'

She smiled, getting into this in a big way. 'Yeah, sentimental old movies. I can just see you in front of a roaring log fire watching Mary Poppins——'

He pulled the car to a halt, laughter teasing in his eyes, and turned to her. 'Absolutely nuts. Right, let's go and see Colin.'

They found the senior partner on his back in bed, and, according to his harassed-looking wife, he was not taking his convalescence well.

Nor, apparently, was there any improvement.

He lifted his head off the pillow, growled a greeting at Leo and dropped his head back again with a grunt of pain.

'Not good, eh?'

Colin swore comprehensively, and then noticed Abbie and apologised.

'I'm just so. . .' Words—respectable ones at least—failed him, and he subsided with a sigh. 'My toes are numb,' he reported in disgust.

'Really?' Leo peeled back the bedclothes and did a few neurological tests on his feet, and shook his head, clearly unimpressed.

'I think you're going to need surgery,' he told his senior partner frankly. 'It's getting worse, Colin, not better. How are you when you get up to use the bathroom?'

He gave a snort of disgust. 'I crawl on my hands and knees. Megan has to help me up—it's awful.'

'He's stopped drinking—he has scarcely any fluid, just so he doesn't have to go to the loo. It's crazy, Leo.'

Leo nodded thoughtfully. 'Look, I'll ring the orthopods and have a word—who do you want to see?'

'Graeme Brown's the back chap, really.'

'I thought you didn't like him?'

'I don't, but he's a bloody good surgeon.'

Leo grinned. 'OK, I'll contact him. Will you see him privately?'

'I'll do it as fast as possible—if that means privately, so be it. I can't stand this much more.'

'OK. I suspect he'll admit you later today and operate tomorrow. I'll be in touch—oh, and pick up a bottle and a bedpan from the surgery, Megan, and get some fluids into him. The last thing he needs is dehydration to complicate things.'

Megan rolled her eyes. 'Don't tell me, Leo—tell him. If there was ever a stubborn ostrich——'

Leo chuckled. 'Don't worry, we'll get him sorted out.'

'I am still in the room, you know,' Colin grumbled from the bed. 'No bedside manner, have you? Now, young Dr Pearce—how are you getting on? This rascal treating you all right? I hope he's not working you too hard and exhausting you.'

Abbie fought the blush. 'He's a very good teacher,' she replied, and caught Leo's eye. He winked broadly, and she pointedly turned away and ignored him. 'He is, however, fixated on role-play exercises.'

Colin chuckled. 'Oh, yes, I know. He makes us all

do it, you know—compulsory in-service training. Every now and again we have a topic we discuss, do some mock-consultations and grade each other on handling the patient, observation of body language and hidden agendas, that sort of thing. He's disgustingly good at it.'

Judging by the sound of it Colin wasn't any keener than Abbie, which would have suited her fine if she could see any likelihood of him returning to the practice in the near future. Unfortunately, however, if he was going to be off for months it was possible that she would have to transfer to another practice—but she'd worry about that if and when it happened.

They left the Williams' house and went back to the surgery, pausing to buy sandwiches from a garage, then they ate them quickly over a cup of coffee before Leo rang the consultant about Colin and Abbie started her antenatal clinic at two.

It was a clinic of contrasts, she thought afterwards. One girl, only nineteen, had conceived by accident and was living at home with her mother, a divorcee.

'All that hassle for a bit of sex,' the girl had said with a bitter laugh, and Abbie was saddened. Saddened for the girl, with her jaded attitude, and saddened most particularly for the unwanted baby. God knows what kind of life it'll have, she'd thought as she'd listened to the tiny heart beating.

Everything, however, was going well, and she'd sent the girl away with instructions to return in four weeks.

By contrast the next patient, Jenny Dobson, was a woman in her late thirties who had been offered amniocentesis and declined it.

'I'd be unable to have a termination anyway, so I

might just as well tough it out. After all, there's a risk of losing a perfectly healthy baby after amniocentesis, and we both wanted this one so much, it didn't seem sensible to risk it.'

'Have you been trying long?' Abbie asked as she felt gently round the swollen abdomen.

'Eight years. I couldn't believe it when it happened. We'd just gone through all the adoption business, having tried all the other avenues and decided against IVF—well, it seems such a lot of heartache and it seems to work in so few cases. Anyway, we'd decided to adopt, been interviewed by the agency and approved, and then Ian said we ought to go on holi-day—last one as a couple and all that, and booked us into the honeymoon suite!'

She laughed. 'It was wonderful, very relaxed and so romantic, and for the first time we felt there was no pressure on us, no possible outcome to our perform-ance—we actually enjoyed ourselves for the first time in about eight years, and this is the result!'

Abbie smiled. 'A genuine happy ending—how marvellous.'

'Oh, it is—I just hope everything's all right. I couldn't bear it if something went wrong now.'

Abbie folded the stethoscope and tucked it into her pocket. 'Of course there are no guarantees, but every-thing does seem to be going well at the moment and there's no reason to suppose it won't continue to do so. When are you due?'

'End of October—nine weeks.'

Abbie nodded. 'Right, well, let's see you again in a fortnight and we'll see how you are then, but I don't expect there'll be any problems. Where are you booked to have the baby?'

Mrs Dobson bit her lip. 'Would you think I was very foolish if I opted for a home delivery?'

Abbie perched on the edge of the couch and regarded her thoughtfully. 'Really? The truth? I would think that if you're fit and healthy there's probably no reason why you shouldn't, but then, having said that, the nearest hospital is half an hour away and if anything goes wrong—well. . . I mean, every baby is precious, but this one seems to have been so elusive and means so much to you, would you really be prepared to risk what might be your last chance?'

Jenny Dobson gave a rueful smile. 'That's what Ian said. I suppose you can't both be wrong.'

Abbie smiled and straightened up. 'We could, but I think on balance we probably aren't. What did Dr Williams say?'

'Hospital,' she said emphatically, and they laughed.

'Well, there you are, then. That's three of us.'

'Four, really,' she confessed. 'I tend to agree with you all. Having the baby at home is just a romantic notion. I think when it came to it I'd panic and want to go in.'

Abbie discussed her case with Leo later, and asked if she had given the right advice.

He shrugged. 'Maybe. I know them—they live quite near me. She's fit, healthy—there's no reason why anything should go wrong. I'd be inclined to let her try.'

'Yes, but I wouldn't!' Abbie retorted. 'I couldn't live with that on my conscience.'

'What? Letting a patient do what he or she wanted

to? You can only advise, Abbie. If she turned round at the last minute and said she was having the baby at home, all you could do would be to advise against it and write in the notes that it was a home delivery against medical advice. There'd be nothing else you could do. If she decides to have it at home, you're stuck.'

'Hmm. I'd just have to hope the baby wasn't!'

He shrugged again. 'They seldom are. Babies are remarkably good at being born — it's what they do best. What are you doing after surgery?'

'Going home to bed.'

His eyes sparkled with interest. 'Oh, good.'

'Alone.'

'Not so good. Could I be allowed to talk you out of it?'

'Or yourself into it?'

'Absolutely.'

She laughed despite her best attempts. 'No. Watch my lips; N.O.'

'Why?'

She looked away. 'Because I'm shattered.'

His hand trailed slowly down her arm, then back up again, teasing her senses. 'Are you sure I can't persuade you otherwise? I'll cook for you.' His voice was soft, coaxing. She didn't need a great deal of persuading — having spent the weekend being subjected to his cooking, she was confident that it would be an excellent meal.

Unfortunately he was rather good at everything he did, and she was very much afraid that it would become addictive.

And if Colin was off for a long time. . .

'What happened about Dr Williams?'

'He's gone in—laminectomy tomorrow. Don't change the subject.'

'Please, Leo, I'm worried about it. What if he's off for ages?'

'You mean your status as a trainee?' His shoulders lifted slightly. 'You might have to move to another practice if he's going to be off for several months. Otherwise it should be OK. Why? Afraid you'll miss me?'

She snorted. 'Your ego's showing again, Dr Chandler.'

'Come for supper, Dr Pearce.'

She shook her head. 'No, really, I ought to do some work——'

'I've got a lovely bit of fillet steak——'

'No!'

'—and mushrooms, and cherry tomatoes and fresh green beans and some late new potatoes from the garden——'

'No!'

'—and a bottle of claret, and some soft music, and a wonderfully comfortable bed with just enough room for both of us——'

She put her hands over her ears and shook her head.

'I'll test you on treatment of congestive heart failure in the elderly,' he coaxed, his voice softly sing-song, and Abbie groaned in despair.

'Leo, stop it.'

He grinned. 'Tempting you yet?'

She gave a rueful little smile. 'Got any raspberries and cream?'

He nodded slowly.

'Oh, blast,' she sighed, and he tugged her into his arms and chuckled in triumph.

'Knew I could do it!' he crowed, and she thumped him on the arm and wriggled free.

'You're a beast.'

'Grr.'

She giggled and slipped out of reach, turning to find Ravi standing there in the doorway, arms folded, eyes like rapiers.

'Kids,' she said in disgust.

'You're just jealous, Ravinda,' Leo told her with what Abbie thought was incredible tactlessness considering it was probably true.

Ravi, however, laughed. 'No way, Chandler. I have bigger fish to fry.'

Leo lounged against the table. 'So I hear — ENT man. Lot's of nice private practice — congratulations.'

Ravi peered down her nose at him. 'Really, Leo — he's a very nice guy. You might at least wish us well.'

'It's that serious, is it?'

She shrugged. 'I hope so. Maybe. Time will undoubtedly tell.'

Leo looked at her in amazement. 'Not wedding-bells, surely?'

Ravi laughed. 'You don't have to say it as though it's some foul disease.'

'Sorry — it's just that I wouldn't have thought you were the type.'

'Well, you never did find the time to discover just what type I was, did you?' she said cryptically. 'Still, all water under the bridge now. Actually, I want a favour. Will you swap duty nights with me? I'm supposed to be on tonight and Richard's just rung and asked me out — some posh dinner somewhere. I said yes before I remembered.'

'Sorry,' Leo said without the slightest sign of penitence. 'I'm busy tonight.'

Ravi shot Abbie a half-smile. 'I'm sure Abbie will give you a rain-check, Leo — after all, she was extraordinarily reluctant. . .'

Abbie, caught between the two of them, shrugged. 'Don't use me as an excuse or a lever, please. I'm happy either way.'

Leo clearly was not, but agreed on one condition — that Ravi do his Saturday morning surgery as well.

'You're a gem,' Ravi told him. 'Hard as a rock, but decorative enough to be desirable.'

Abbie laughed. 'Sounds right to me.'

'I get the distinct impression I'm being ganged up on here,' he grumbled gently, and, straightening, he ambled past Abbie, dropping a kiss on her lips, then patted Ravi on the cheek. 'Women — I must be nuts.'

Abbie found herself alone then with her arch-rival, and didn't quite know what to say.

It turned out to be easy, and Ravi turned out to be much more human than Abbie had believed.

'Thank you for agreeing to the swap,' she said, and to Abbie's surprise she looked quite sincere. 'It was a mean trick, and I don't suppose you were that reluctant at all to have dinner with him tonight, but I am really very grateful.'

Abbie smiled at her. 'Think nothing of it; I'd be quite glad of an early night.'

'Ah, yes — after your hectic weekend with our voracious young doctor. It won't hurt him to be dangled on a string for a while, Abbie. Take my advice — don't let him get his own way all the time. He won't respect you for it.'

Abbie didn't quite know how to reply to that, but fortunately she was spared the necessity because Ravi turned in the doorway and went back out, leaving her alone with her thoughts——

Not least of which was that she was intensely disappointed that she would not, after all, be seeing Leo tonight.

CHAPTER SEVEN

THEIR evening together was, in fact, postponed until
Thursday — by which time Simon Partridge had come
back complaining that his sore throat was no better and
now he had stomach pains.

Abbie patiently examined him, growing more
uncomfortable by the minute, particularly when Simon
took her hand in his cool, damp one.

'It hurts in here,' he explained, squashing her palm
against his abdomen, 'and here, sometimes.'

'Are you constipated?' Abbie asked bluntly, and he
blinked. Clearly such an unromantic topic was more
than he was prepared to discuss — but then, if he
refused. . .

Abbie could almost hear his mind working. Finally
he coughed and shook his head.

'No — not that I'm aware of. I might be, though,' he
added almost hopefully.

'I'm sure you'd know,' Abbie told him, her voice
dry. However, to satisfy him she poked and prodded,
considered doing a rectal examination to embarrass
him into retreat and then thought better of it. What if
he really wasn't well?

She made him dress again and went over his eating
habits and other possible causes of pain — like a strain
injury, eating out — anything that could cause otherwise
symptomless pain.

There was no redness, no rebound tenderness, no

raised blood-pressure or temperature—nothing, in fact, to give her any clue as to what might be wrong with him.

In the back of her mind, though, was pain from the spleen or adrenals as a result of mild glandular fever—but there was no way she was going to poke about feeling for enlarged glands in his groin! There were none in the neck or throat, and no pain that he had complained of in the armpits, so she was fairly confident that he was just time-wasting.

However, to cover herself she took a blood sample to test for mononucleosis and sent him on his way.

She told Leo about it that night as they ate the meal he had cooked for them, and he shook his head and sighed.

'He's going to be a damn nuisance, isn't he? Perhaps we ought to ask Jackie to refer him to me when he next tries to make an appointment. That should stop him. Want any more?'

It was a delicious casserole, packed with vegetables from the garden, and Abbie had already eaten more than she could comfortably cope with. She shook her head.

'I don't think I could—not if I'm going to do the raspberries justice!'

'Ah, the raspberries,' he said with a lazy smile. 'They're in the bedroom.'

Her eyes widened slightly. 'The bedroom?'

He said nothing, merely reaching out his hand. 'Shall we go and have our dessert?'

The meaning in his eyes was clear, and Abbie's heart thumped against her ribs. Did he have direct access to it? she thought numbly as she let him pull her out of the seat and towards the stairs.

Certainly he had direct access to her will, because there was no thought of resistance in her mind.

A bottle of home-made peach wine stood open on the bedside table, next to a brimming bowl of juicy raspberries and another bowl of rich, thick cream.

'Um — there are no spoons,' she said weakly.

'No.'

He tugged her blouse out of her jeans and unbuttoned it with slow, lazy fingers, then he slid it off her shoulders, leaving her wrists shackled. His fingers traced the outline of her bra, teasing the soft skin of her breasts and making her nipples strain against the lace. He found the clip between her breasts and released them, cupping them in his warm palms with a sigh of satisfaction. 'Oh, Abigail. . .'

He lowered his head, brushing the pale slopes with the slight rasp of his jaw, then soothing the skin with hot, open-mouthed kisses that made her legs buckle.

'Leo, please,' she whispered, and he lifted his head and stared deep into her eyes.

'Beautiful,' he rasped, and then turned her round, freeing her wrists of the shirt and tossing it into the corner before stripping off the rest of her clothes. His own followed, flung heedlessly on to the pile, and then he lifted her and dropped her into the centre of the bed, straddling her hips.

'Now — about the dessert.' He reached across and plucked a raspberry from the bowl, immersed it in the cream and then held it out to her.

This time she knew what to do, drawing his fingers into her mouth and caressing them one by one with her tongue. A muscle jumped in his jaw, and he pulled his fingers away and picked up another raspberry, dropping it into her tummy button.

'What are you doing?' she squeaked, and then gasped as he bent forward and chased it out with his tongue, driving her wild with need.

'Leo,' she moaned, and he laughed, a soft, husky chuckle.

'Oh, sexy, sexy lady. You're delicious. . .'

His mouth marauded gently over her body, licking and biting, suckling and soothing, until she was mindless with ecstasy and shaking from head to foot. Then, when she could stand it no more, he rolled on to his back, arms spread, a sensuous challenge in his eyes.

'My turn,' he said softly.

Abbie had a field day. He was beautiful, satin skin over smooth, taut muscles, his rangy frame lean and healthy, his body hers to do with as she would.

She discovered she was even more daring than she had believed possible, and by the time she reached his toes Leo was shaking all over.

She slid a hand back up his leg and he grasped it in his, hauling her up his body until they were lying face to face.

'Now, Abbie,' he growled, and she was only too ready to oblige.

Being in control gave her a power over him that was shatteringly sweet, and when the harsh shudders of release racked his body she fell headlong into the wild storm, collapsing against him with a sobbing cry.

As the tremors passed, Abbie opened her eyes and moved her head a little so that she could see him.

He was looking at her, a slightly quizzical expression

on his face, as if he couldn't quite believe what had happened.

'God, Abbie,' he groaned, and a slow, satisfied grin quirked his lips. 'You are one hell of a woman.'

She searched his face, seeing tenderness in his eyes. 'I love you,' she said softly.

He groaned again, turning his head away.

'No, Abbie; don't do this to us.'

She sat up. 'Do what?' She reached out and turned his face back towards her. 'Do what?' she repeated.

'Sanitise our lovemaking — why can't you just accept it for what it is?'

She swallowed the hurt. 'That's exactly what I am doing, Leo — accepting it for what it is. For me, at least. I can't speak for you, I know that, and I'm not asking you to feel the same. If you don't, you don't, but you can't deny me the right to my feelings any more than you can dictate them to me. And I do love you.'

He sighed and lifted her off him, swinging his legs over the bed and walking to the window. After a few moments he sighed sharply and ran his hands through his hair. 'This is crazy,' he informed her. 'If you allow yourself to believe it, you'll just get hurt.'

She gave a hollow laugh. 'Oh, I think that's inevitable anyway. I always knew that, Leo. It's just that sometimes we do things that aren't very wise as a sort of calculated risk. Having an affair with you was a calculated risk. I lost. My fault.'

She slid off the bed and walked over to him, resting her hand on his shoulder. 'It doesn't make any difference to our relationship. If it makes you uncomfortable, I won't say it. It doesn't change anything.'

He stood there for a while, his back to her, saying nothing, then he turned slowly and stared down into her eyes.

'I didn't want you to get hurt, Abbie. You won't change me. I'm a bachelor — and very happy that way. This is an affair, nothing more, nothing less. When it ends, it's over. And it will end, make no mistake.'

She lowered her eyes to mask the pain she knew must show in them, and nodded. 'I know,' she said, her voice small and hurt-sounding despite her best attempt. She drew in a deep breath to banish the threatening tears, and turned back towards the bed.

'How about these raspberries?'

She climbed into the bed, piled the pillows up against the headboard and waited.

He gave a heavy sigh and followed her, reaching across her for the bowls and balancing them on their knees. 'Open your mouth.'

He fed her, in a curiously gentle gesture that had nothing sexual about it, rather more nurturing, as if he was trying to make amends for hurting her, and when he finally put the bowls down and pulled her into his arms his caresses were tender, his body caring. Even the end was gentle, her cries muted, and when a tear slid out of the corner of her eye he wiped it tenderly away.

'Oh, Abbie, I'm sorry,' he murmured, and she knew he was hurting too.

That gave her hope. . .

He took her home that night, and every subsequent night.

It was as if he was afraid to let her get too close, in

case she became too firmly entrenched in his home —
and his heart.

She wasn't sure if he loved her. She thought probably
not, but she got the distinct impression that he was
fighting it.

Hence the business of taking her home. If she stayed,
it could so easily turn into living together, and,
although he pointed out, quite justifiably, that because
she lived in the town centre it wouldn't look good for
her to be missing all night, it didn't explain the equally
prejudicial fact of her arriving back in the wee small
hours, nor did it take into account the lingering goodbye kisses in her flat, or the fact that sometimes he
even stayed for more than just kisses.

But just as she never spent the night at his cottage,
so he always left her flat before dawn.

Abbie contented herself with the situation, confident
that by the end of the year she would have won him
round — assuming she could survive in general practice
that long, which was by no means a foregone
conclusion.

Simon Partridge continued to come in, refusing to
see anyone else, and presenting her with nothing more
concrete than the odd pain here and there and the
persistent sore throat.

'I've got a cure for his throat,' Leo said drily one
afternoon towards the end of the following week. 'Slit
it.'

Abbie gave a startled laugh. 'Leo, that's awful!'

'Oh, God, he's wasting so much of your time! Next
time he comes, refer him to me, eh?'

Jackie, the receptionist, popped her head round the

door. 'Mrs Willis rang,' she told Leo. 'She's got chest pain again.'

'So send Ravi—she's on call.'

Jackie shrugged. 'She won't go.'

Leo shoved back the chair and stood up. 'Bloody woman. Coming?'

Abbie nodded, screwed the lid on her pen and followed him out.

They went in his car—the Volvo this time—and pulled up outside Mrs Willis's house to find a cluster of people round the gate.

'Collapsed in the front garden,' one of them said. 'Poor old duck—we couldn't lift her back inside. Jimmy thinks she's dead, Doc.'

Jimmy was crouched beside the recumbent form of Mrs Willis, and looked up as the crowd parted to let them through.

'Too late, Doc—she's gone,' he told Leo.

'OK, could we have a bit of room, please?' Leo said to the crowd, and they moved back a pace or two. He knelt on the weedy path beside her, and felt in her neck for a pulse, but there was none.

With a sigh Leo shrugged his jacket off and laid it gently over her face.

'All right, folks, the show's over. Let's have a little respect for her, please.'

They faded away, leaving only a small boy huddled in a corner of the garden, his eyes huge.

'I didn't do it, really I didn't,' he said tearfully.

Abbie looked up at him, puzzled. 'Didn't do what, sweetheart?' she asked gently.

'Kill her—I didn't, really.'

'Of course you didn't kill her. She was a very sick

lady.' She studied him thoughtfully for a second, then asked, 'What made you think you might have done?'

A tear wobbled on his lower lid. 'She came out. I was playing in the street, and I sneaked up to the gate and said, Boo. She went all funny and fell down then — but I didn't kill her, I didn't.'

The tear splashed down on to his dirty sweatshirt, and he sniffed hard and wiped his nose on the back of his grubby hand.

Abbie put her arm round his trembling shoulders. 'No, love, of course you didn't kill her. She'd already phoned the surgery to say she wasn't feeling well. It was nothing to do with you, but I expect you were very frightened, weren't you?'

He nodded and another tear spilt down his cheek.

'Come on, let's take you home and explain to your mum. It's a big shock the first time you see someone dead. I remember the first time it happened to me. . .'

She steered him round the lifeless Mrs Willis and out into the street, then up the path to his house, talking reassuringly to him all the time.

'Oh, now what's he done, the little devil?' his mother scolded, and Abbie kept her arm round the skinny shoulders and explained the situation.

'Oh, poor little mite—come here,' his mother said, and, crouching down, she wrapped the now sobbing child in her arms. 'Thank you for bringing him home — he's not supposed to go out by himself but he will slip past me when I'm busy and then he's gone —— Well, you won't be in such a hurry to get out next time, will you pet?'

Abbie took her leave to went back to Leo, to find him using his mobile phone to call an ambulance.

Abbie met his eyes over the woman's body.

'Poor old thing,' she said softly.

Leo shrugged. 'She's better off like this. She wasn't at all well, Abbie, and none of her family bothered with her.'

Just then a big ginger cat came miaowing out of the front door and sniffed Mrs Willis's feet curiously before winding round Leo's legs. He scratched its ears absently, and the cat purred and rubbed against him.

'Wonder what will happen to you, puss?' Abbie murmured.

'You could ask the neighbours if they would have him,' Leo suggested, and she straightened just as the net curtain next door twitched shut.

She walked up the path and rang the bell.

A man in his fifties answered the door. 'Yep?' he grunted.

'I wondered if you could help us — it's about the cat —'

'Bloody scavenger — nothing to do with me. Have it put down,' he snapped, and slammed the door in her face.

The neighbour on the other side was friendlier but no more helpful. 'Sorry, love — he's a horror, that one. Always picking fights. Nobody round here'll have him.'

'What about Mrs Willis's children?' Abbie suggested.

The neighbour gave a rude snort. 'Them? They're only interested in what they can get out of her — always have been. Never done a thing for her, not one of them. I did more'n they did. No, love, you'd better take him to the police and have him put in the pound — maybe they can find a new home for him?'

Abbie went back to Leo with the news, and an idea

of her own. 'You could always keep him,' she
suggested.

Leo's eyes widened. 'What? What about when I go
on holiday, or go away for the weekend?'

'I'm sure your gardener would be able to feed him,
or you could put him in a cattery. They're very
independent, cats.'

'So why don't you have him?'

'In a flat? Come on, Leo, it would be cruel.'

Leo groaned in defeat. 'OK, I'll take him back to
the house and keep him for a few days, just until the
family have decided what they want to do with him.'

'Great—I knew you would.' She went back to the
friendly neighbour to tell her the news, and asked the
cat's name.

'Tiger—and he's well-named. Tell Dr Chandler I
wish him luck!'

Abbie grinned. She had no intention of telling Leo
any such thing. His agreement had been reluctant in
the extreme as it was!

The police came then, and Leo explained about
Tiger and the policeman promised to inform the relatives. Then the ambulance arrived and after much
struggling they managed to lift Mrs Willis on to a
stretcher and up into the back of the van. It drove off,
and Leo turned to Abbie.

'Cat?'

'Mmm. How are we going to transport him?'

Leo grinned. 'Your problem—I'm driving.'

In the end she sat in the back and struggled with the
yowling cat all the way to Leo's cottage. Once they
arrived Leo grabbed him from her under the shoulders,

holding him so that his feet were pointing safely in the other direction, and Abbie quickly opened the door.

With an ungrateful squawk Tiger shot out of Leo's arms and dashed up the stairs, and Leo dusted off his hands and turned back to Abbie. She was inspecting the scratches on her hands.

'Ouch,' he said softly, and led her into the kitchen. 'Wash them and I'll put some cream on them.'

'Cream? I need a skin graft,' she grumbled.

'It was your idea,' he reminded her.

'Humph! Damn cat. What about feeding him? He'll need a litter tray, too. Can't let him out for a few days—and he could probably do with being neutered and a set of injections——'

'Hang on a goddam minute there,' Leo growled. 'This cat is here under protest for the shortest possible time. He is not, and never will be, a permanent resident!'

'Of course not,' Abbie said calmly. 'But in the meantime he needs food and a litter tray.'

While Abbie opened a tin of salmon—'Spoilt cat,' Leo muttered—he went out into the greenhouse and came back with a seed tray full of soil.

'That will have to do him for now,' he said, and went upstairs to find the cat curled up in the middle of his bed, fast asleep.

'Come on, monster—downstairs with you.'

The cat wiggled in vain, and in seconds Leo had him shut in the kitchen with the food and litter and they were on their way back to the surgery.

'Damn cat.'

'He's lovely.'

Leo shot her a jaundiced look. 'Temporary home, right?'

She smiled sweetly. 'Of course, Leo, dear.'

He grunted, but Abbie was well-content. Even Leo hadn't been able to resist giving the cat a last stroke before shutting him up.

She'd have him domesticated yet.

On the work front things were going less well. Colin Williams was back home following his laminectomy, and was still in quite a lot of pain. Clearly it was going to be some considerable time before he was back to work, and that of course begged the question of whether Abbie would be able to continue her training in the practice. The one thing in her favour was the fact that she was helping to share the extra workload, although she was very conscious of the fact that she carried less than her fair share.

Even so she was exhausted, and the arrival of her period did nothing to improve her stamina.

It did, however, give her the opportunity to go on the Pill, which she did.

She told Leo, thinking he would be pleased as it meant he would be freed of the responsibility. Instead he told her it was unnecessary, and she wondered then if it was because it gave their relationship a sense of permanence that he was desperately trying to avoid.

It didn't, however, prevent him from taking advantage of the situation as soon as possible, and Abbie found that the absence of any barriers unbelievably gave their lovemaking even greater intimacy.

She was much more comfortable now with her responses, and, provided she kept her mouth shut on those three little words, Leo was tender and loving with her. It didn't stop her behaviour from being loving, but he seemed to be able to cope with that — or perhaps it was just easier to ignore.

The thing — or rather person — impossible to ignore was Simon Partridge.

He came again, on the Monday morning ten days after Mrs Willis had died, and this time complained of a pain in the groin.

No way was Abbie being drawn into that.

'You know, Mr Partridge,' she told him seriously, 'I'm very worried about you. I can't seem to find anything wrong with you, but then I haven't got a great deal of experience in general practice. I think we ought to ask Dr Chandler to take a look at you, just to be on the safe side. After all, I'd hate to miss anything vital out of inexperience.' She all but batted her lashes at him, and turned to the phone. 'Dr Chandler? Dr Pearce here. I've got Mr Partridge with me, and he seems to have a pain in the groin —— '

Leo snorted down the phone, and Abbie hid her smile. 'That's right. I quite agree, so I wonder if you could have a look at him?'

'I'll be in in a minute.'

The phone crashed back on the hook, and a moment later Leo tapped on the door and ambled in.

'Right, Mr Partridge, I gather you've been having all sorts of funny aches and pains. Better have a look, hadn't we? Just pop all your clothes off for me.'

His eyes widened. 'All of them?' he asked, clearly stunned.

'Please, if you wouldn't mind? Thank you.'

Leo yanked the curtain closed around the cubicle

and winked at Abbie. 'Leave him to me,' he mouthed. 'You just sit there and I'll sort him out.'

'Um—I'm ready,' the man said hesitantly, and Leo yanked back the curtain.

'Jolly good—right, then, let's have a look. Stand up, please.'

He put the man, who became more and more embarrassed by the second, through all manner of increasingly intrusive examinations and procedures, until in the end Abbie was convinced he must have checked every last orifice the man possessed.

Then he stripped off his gloves, closed the curtain and told him to get dressed.

Abbie was controlling her laughter with the most enormous difficulty, and Leo's cheerful grin did nothing to help.

Finally the man emerged from behind the screen, sheepish in the extreme, and Leo pasted on a professional smile.

'Well, Mr Partridge, whatever it was must have cleared up, I think, because I couldn't find a thing wrong with you. However, we could, of course, admit you to hospital for further testing——'

'No, no, I expect you're right, Doctor,' the man mumbled unhappily, and left as fast as was decently possible without once catching Abbie's eye.

As the door closed behind him the giggle escaped, and Leo sat on the edge of the desk and chuckled.

'Poor man,' Abbie said eventually, wiping the tears from her eyes. 'Was there a place you didn't check?'

Leo grinned. 'Just being thorough. I don't think he'll trouble you again, my dear. Oh, after you've finished could you go and have a word with Mary Tanner? She phoned this morning and it was you she particularly wanted to see.'

'Sure. Any idea what about?'

Leo shook his head. 'No, none, but if you aren't sure about anything just tell her so and come back to me. I'm sure she won't mind. Maybe she just wants a woman doctor to talk to. Can you find the way?'

'Yes, I think so. I'll take the address and I've got a map. Is she still at home?'

'Oh, yes—it may be about going back into the hospice for drug review, or further radiotherapy to halt the pain. The community nurses said she was struggling a bit, and any more morphine makes her nauseated.'

'Could the hospice take her?'

'Depends on their bed state. Check before you go.'

'OK.'

She had got to know the staff at St Saviour well in the past few weeks, and when she rang she was told that there would be no problem if Mary needed to go back. In fact they were almost expecting her to.

When Abbie arrived at the house the door was opened by a neighbour who had come in to sit with her for a while. She took advantage of Abbie's arrival to go, and Mary was clearly relieved. 'She means well but she just doesn't know what to say to me,' she explained. 'It's so wearing.'

'I'm sure. What can I do for you?'

'Oh——' Mary shrugged her slight shoulders and sighed. 'I'm losing weight, and I'm getting breathless, and the pain seems to be coming back. The radiotherapist seemed to think he could only do so much, and I don't know if I can be bothered going through it for such a short time.'

Abbie took her hand. 'Do you feel it's going to be a short time, now?'

Mary nodded. 'Yes, I do. I feel—different. More accepting, somehow.'

'Would you like to go back into the hospice for a bit?'

She chewed her lip. 'I would, but only for a few days. The trouble is, I don't think the girls are too keen on me dying at home.'

Abbie studied her, and saw the sad resignation in her eyes. 'Is that what you'd like to do? Die at home?'

Mary nodded. 'It would seem right, somehow. It's where I belong.' She sighed softly. 'I don't want to make it harder for the others, though. They have to go on afterwards, and if the memory of my death will haunt them—well, I just couldn't do that to them.'

'Have you talked to them about it?'

She shook her head. 'They won't talk about it. Gerry will, and he says he's happy about it, but the girls——'

She sighed again, and her eyes drifted shut. 'It's so hard to please everyone, and I haven't got the energy to fight for what I want, especially when I don't feel I have the right to ask it of them.'

Abbie didn't know what to say. It was such a complex and difficult issue, and it needed time and thought and discussion in order to bring about a happy solution. All she could do at that time was listen and let Mary talk, and that Mary did, dozing intermittently.

Clearly her stamina was fading. Abbie took her pulse and found it light and a little fast, like her respiration. She was obviously nearing the end, and Abbie felt sure that it would only be a few more weeks, if that.

Mary drifted back again then, and smiled wearily at

Abbie. 'Gerry's been wonderful the last three weeks. He went and spoke to Leo, and since then—well, he's been much more accepting. Before that I couldn't talk to him at all, but now we can cry about it together.' She looked towards the window, but it was clear that she was seeing a different view.

'We've started making love again. We stopped for a long time, and Gerry kept making excuses to avoid it, but since he saw Leo he's been much better able to cope with emotion. It's almost as if he's been given the OK to have feelings.' She laughed softly. 'I'm so grateful to him—he gave me my husband back, just in the nick of time. We've shared so much in the past few weeks. It's been like falling in love all over again, only without that terrible urgency. It's so much more peaceful, but still the feelings are just as strong, if not stronger. I feel so close when we make love—as if nothing can touch us. Does that sound crazy?'

Abbie shook her head. 'No, no, that doesn't sound crazy at all. I know exactly what you mean.'

Mary looked at her keenly. 'You're having an affair with Leo, aren't you?'

Abbie blinked, and was on the point of denying it when the absurdity of it shook her. Here was this woman—all right, she was a patient, but she was sharing the most intimate secrets of her life, and her thoughts about her imminent death, and Abbie was about to deny her relationship with Leo? *That* was crazy. She nodded.

'Yes—yes, I am.'

'He's a funny guy—can I give you a word of advice?'

Abbie laughed softly. 'Frankly, I'd be glad of any advice I could get!'

'Don't let him have it all his own way. He's too used to it, and he thinks he likes it that way, but it isn't good for people not to compromise.' She grinned. 'I saw the way he was looking at you — you'd have to be blind and deaf not to notice. And, OK, you could have an affair and leave it at that, but you aren't like that, are you, Abbie? Can I call you Abbie?'

She nodded. 'Of course — and no, I'm not like that. Not at all.' A little sigh escaped her. 'I love him. I made the mistake of telling him that once. Not a smart move.'

Mary chuckled softly. 'I can imagine — I should think it completely freaked him out. I think you'll have to give him time, and plenty of it, before you'll be able to trap him. He'll have to be so far in he won't realise the net's closing.' She grinned. 'If he knew we were planning his downfall, he'd probably become a staunch advocate of euthanasia!'

They laughed together, then Mary sobered. 'I suppose I ought to go back into the hospice, but I'm loath to do it until the girls will accept me back at home again.'

'Are you afraid they won't let you leave the hospice and that you'll die there?'

Mary nodded, her eyes filling up. 'I want to be here. I know the hospice is wonderful, and for many people it's the only answer, but I couldn't bear to —' She broke off, unable to speak, and Abbie held her hand and waited until she had control again.

'Can I talk to them tonight after school? Maybe then I'll be able to go in.'

'How about the hospice staff talking to them? They have nurse counsellors on the staff who are wonderful,

who could help them face their fears—or they could
see a psychotherapist or someone from Cruse, the
bereavement care charity. Maybe you're just too close.'

'But I'm their mother!'

'Exactly. How can they tell you that they're angry
that you're dying, that they won't accept that you are,
that they're afraid of how things will change without
you? Maybe, like Gerry, talking to someone else will
help to unlock the fears and get them out into the open
so they can deal with them.'

'Oh, I hope so,' she sighed. 'I really hope so, because
I'm wasting all the time I have left with them because
they just won't talk to me any more. . .'

She bit her lip to stop the tears, but they fell anyway,
in torrents, and Abbie stayed with her and made her a
cup of tea and waited until the nurse came.

'I have to dash—I've got a clinic—but I'll talk to
Leo and the hospice and see what we can come up
with,' she promised.

She had to race back to the surgery for her antenatal
clinic, and by the time it was finished it was time for
her evening surgery.

It was nearly seven before she had a chance to talk
to Leo, and he took one look at her and told her he'd
follow her home.

Once in the little flat she turned into his arms and
hugged him hard.

'Mary?' he said softly, and she nodded.

'The kids won't accept it. What can we do for them?'

'There's a counsellor attached to the hospice—Sarah
Rudd. I'll get her to give them a ring. Can I use your
phone?'

He rang her there and then, and within minutes had

arranged for the woman to visit the Tanners that evening.

'Now,' he said to Abbie. 'You need a shower, a long, cool drink and a hug, in the reverse order. Come here.'

She went.

CHAPTER EIGHT

MARY TANNER died peacefully at home three weeks later.

Gerry rang Abbie early on the Saturday morning. He had tried Leo's number but he was out, and he wondered if one of them could come because he felt sure the end was near.

Abbie went via Leo's house and found him just getting out of his car.

'Gerry Tanner just phoned. He thinks Mary's dying,' she told him.

'Oh, hell,' Leo sighed. 'Right, I'll go round. Are you coming?'

Abbie didn't hesitate. She had become very close to Mary over the previous few weeks, and it seemed right to be there at the end.

They went in Leo's car, and let themselves into the house as Gerry had instructed. They found him and the two girls sitting by Mary's side in the little room downstairs that had become her bedroom.

She was still alive, but only just, her breathing very light, her face pale but composed.

'She seemed to go into a coma at about six this morning,' Gerry told them quietly. 'I don't think she's really aware of us any more.'

'She may be — hearing is the last thing to go. Talk to her — say the things you want to say. She can't respond any more, but I think she may well be able to hear.

Why don't you take turns and spend a few minutes alone with her?'

Gerry nodded, and suggested that Clare, the oldest girl, should go first.

'I don't want to be alone with her!' she whispered, her eyes wide. 'What if——' She was unable to finish the sentence, to put her fears into words, so Leo did, very gently.

'She won't die for a little while, Clare. You're quite safe with her—she's your mother.'

Clare stared at him for a moment, then nodded.

'OK.'

They left her, and a few minutes later she came out, sobbing.

'Shall I go?' Josephine asked.

Her father nodded, and she went in but left the door open a crack. They could hear her talking, very softly, then she came out, dry-eyed but very sober.

'Your turn, Dad.'

Gerry stared at the ceiling. 'Oh, God.'

'Go on,' Leo urged. 'We'll look after the girls.'

After a few minutes in which the girls waited, sitting side by side and clinging to each other's hands, he came out and leant against the door-post.

'I think she's going,' he said raggedly.

The girls exchanged glances, and he held out his arms and they ran to him. After a big hug he took them back in and Abbie and Leo stayed in the hall, the door open slightly, waiting.

Then there was a tiny sob, and Clare ran past them and up the stairs. Jo followed her, eyes still dry, and looked at them blankly.

'She's—dead?'

A harsh, dry sob rose in her throat, and Abbie gathered her into her arms and held her, rocking her while she wept.

Leo went upstairs to Clare, and Abbie could hear him talking, but after a few moments he came back down.

'I think she needs to be alone for a while.'

'What about Gerry?'

Leo shrugged. 'Leave him with Mary.'

His voice sounded harsh and scrapy, and Abbie looked at him in surprise. His cheeks were wet, his eyes glittering. 'Damn,' he whispered, and turned away, fighting his feelings.

Abbie had given up fighting hers. She felt angry, sad, glad that it was over and they could all get on, and yet disbelieving that the funny, gutsy, sparky person that was Mary could have been snuffed out like a candle.

Tears rolled down her cheeks, and she hugged the little girl in her arms even closer, to comfort both of them.

It was a long while before Gerry came out, his eyes dry and curiously empty.

'Where's Clare?' he asked tonelessly.

'Upstairs in her room,' Leo told him. 'Are you OK?'

He nodded shortly and ran up the stairs two at a time.

'Clare?'

They heard him go into her room, and then the murmur of voices from above.

'I want to go up,' Jo said, and Abbie gave her one last hug and let her go.

'Off you go then. All right, poppet?'

She nodded and gave Abbie a watery smile, then ran up the stairs after her father.

Abbie looked at Leo. 'What now?'

'Nothing very much. I certify her, and when they're ready for her to go I'll call an ambulance. There's no rush.'

'No — no, I don't suppose there is any more.'

She sniffed and rummaged in her pocket for a hankie.

'Here.' Leo thrust one at her and she blew her nose and wiped her cheeks.

'Are you OK?' he asked softly.

'I need a hug,' she told him.

'So do I.'

She went into his arms, and they stood for a while, just holding each other, deep in thought.

Then they went together into the little room where Mary lay, and Leo examined her briefly and wrote out the death certificate.

'She looks very peaceful and beautiful,' Abbie said quietly.

'Yes.'

'I'm glad she was at home. It was where she wanted to be.'

He nodded, and she noticed his eyes were filled with tears again.

'So much for not getting involved with your patients,' she teased gently.

He took a deep breath and shot her a crooked grin. 'You can't help it, can you, in circumstances like this? You'd have to be dead from the neck up not to care.'

They heard movement on the stairs, and turned to see Gerry and the girls in the doorway.

'Can we sit with her for a while? I mean — when will the ambulance come —— ?' Gerry broke off and swore softly, his jaw working.

'Take your time,' Leo said quietly. 'We'll wait in the kitchen — I'll make some tea.'

'Thanks.'

They left the little family alone together, and after some time they came out and Gerry nodded.

'I think — we're ready for her to go now.'

'OK.' Leo pushed a cup of tea towards him. 'Drink this. It's got sugar in it. Girls, here, have a drink.'

'I don't want to,' Clare said unevenly.

'You must — come on. You need it. I'll go and make the call.'

Gerry took the girls in the garden while the ambulance was there, and after it was gone they came back in.

They looked helpless, numb and rather lost, and Abbie's heart ached for them.

After making sure they were all right, Leo and Abbie left them alone and went back to Leo's cottage. They spent the day in the garden, Leo mowing the lawn, Abbie picking fruit and making pounds of jam that no one would eat, then in the evening they went to bed and made love with a desperation that left them both shaken and emotionally drained.

She stayed that night, turning to Leo again and again, as if it was imperative that they prove they were still alive.

On Sunday afternoon, though, Leo sent her back to her flat, saying he had work to do and had to go into the surgery.

'I'll see you tomorrow,' he told her, and she got into

her little car and drove back to the town centre, bewildered by his change in attitude. It was as if he was determined to prove to himself that he didn't need her, although his desperation of the night before was frankly more convincing.

Maybe he was beginning to realise what she meant to him, and was fighting it, Abbie thought. That would explain his attitude and behaviour.

Oh, well, she shrugged, and cleaned her flat. It was overdue for doing and high time she tackled it anyway, so perhaps it was just as well to spend some time without him.

Mary's death marked a permanent change in Leo's behaviour. Where before he had been tender and affectionate after their lovemaking, now he seemed to need to distance himself. More often than not they made love at her flat after spending an evening in a local pub or restaurant, and Leo would leave almost immediately.

It was as if he despised the part of him that needed Abbie and couldn't wait to get away. And it hurt.

Many times she cried herself to sleep, and she found it hard to reconcile his behaviour with the light-hearted, friendly person he was at work.

They went to Mary Tanner's funeral on the Friday after her death, and Abbie noticed that Clare was dry-eyed and remote, as if she was holding herself in.

'Denial,' Leo said afterwards. 'I wondered how she would cope. I think we need to watch her.'

Leo should know all about denial, Abbie thought sadly. If only there was a way to get him to admit he cared for her!

But it was hopeless. The only time he showed any emotion was in their dark and stormy lovemaking, and all other contact was light-hearted and trivial.

'Someone came in with a painful eye this morning,' she told him after surgery during the following week.

'Doctor, every time I drink a cup of tea I get a pain in my left eye.'

'Try taking the spoon out,' they said in unison, and she shook her head in despair.

'Will you be serious for a minute?'

'Glaucoma?' he suggested.

'Could be—he's a diabetic.'

'Hmm. Refer him to the clinic.'

'I have.'

'Good. So, what's the problem?'

She sighed. 'No problem. I was just checking that I'd done the right thing.'

'You have no faith in yourself, have you?' he said thoughtfully.

'No. You know that. I hate general practice.'

'Still?'

She lifted her shoulders in a helpless little gesture. 'There are just so many different things all the time— it doesn't seem to matter how many of these ghastly role-play training sessions you make me do, the next surgery there's another case I don't know how to deal with.'

He sighed and pursed his lips. 'You can always ask me, Abbie—pick up the phone and check the answer.'

'But it does nothing for the confidence of the patient! I ought to *know*! Anyway, that isn't what worries me. What really freaks me out is the times I don't realise I've done the wrong thing or missed something.'

He shook his head. 'Abbie, you are a good doctor. You're sincere, you listen well, you're caring—you've got a lot going for you.'

'But not in general practice.'

Leo studied her seriously for a moment. 'I think you're wrong. I think once you got your confidence you'd be a very good GP.'

'I'd be overrun with cats, though,' she pointed out gently.

'Hmm. That blasted cat—temporary, you told me. He's dominating my life at the moment—do you know he sleeps on the bed? In it, sometimes. I have to keep turfing him out because he strops his claws on my leg!'

She chuckled. 'You should close your bedroom door.'

'I don't like it closed.'

'You don't like your leg being flayed to shreds,' she pointed out, and he chuckled.

'What have you got this afternoon?'

She sighed. 'My antenatal clinic, and Jenny Dobson's coming—unless she's had the baby. She's supposed to be due in a couple of weeks, but she seems big for her dates.'

'Want me to have a look at her?'

'Will you be here this afternoon?'

'Should be. Ravi's on duty today. I was going to catch up on some paperwork for Colin.'

'How is he?'

'Grim.'

'Will I have to move to another practice?'

He shrugged. 'I don't know. Possibly, if it goes on much longer. I hope you don't, just when you're finding your feet.'

She sighed. 'Am I, though? I can't help feeling I'd be better off in one branch of medicine, specialising in one type of ailment. You know what's coming then, and you can really get your teeth into it. General practice always seems a real jack-of-all-trades sort of thing, except that you have to be master of all of them, and I just can't do it. I'm not bright enough.'

'Oh, rubbish,' he dismissed. 'You're perfectly bright — you're just scatty.'

'Humph! Want some sandwiches from the bakery?'

'Yes — I'll walk up with you. Ready?'

She picked up her bag, glad to get out into the open air.

It was the beginning of October and there was a nip in the air, but the sky was clear and when they were in the sun it was really very pleasant.

As they walked Abbie thought about the town, and the people in it she had met and come to know, both as patients and as tradespeople in the shops around her flat.

She would miss them and Brocklingford, she realised, if she had to leave. Still, if Colin was unwell and she had no choice, perhaps it would help her to make a decision about the direction of her future.

In the meantime, it was something to bear in mind.

Jenny Dobson was still pregnant but bigger than ever. 'I can't believe I'm going to keep on growing another two weeks!' she said incredulously, staring down at her enormous bump. It wriggled, and she smiled indulgently. 'Little fidget — sometimes it feels as if there are at least two in there.'

Abbie looked at her sharply. 'You have had a scan, haven't you?'

She laughed. 'Oh, yes — I'm only joking. No, there's only one. Pity, twins would have been nice, but. . .' She grinned. 'Still, we'll see. I expect this one will put me off when it arrives.'

'Would you mind if Dr Chandler had a look at you? I don't want to leave you too long before admitting you to hospital. I know you've booked into the GP unit, but even so I'd be reluctant to let you hang on if there was a possibility your dates were wrong.'

'They said the baby was quite small when they did the scan — perhaps there's just a lot of fluid?' She gave a little Gallic shrug. 'Ask Dr Chandler, by all means. I'm in your hands, Dr Pearce. So long as the baby's OK, I don't care what you do really!'

Abbie rang Leo in his surgery and a few moments later he strolled in with a tape-measure in his hand.

'Hmm,' he said thoughtfully, staring at Jenny's bump. 'Well, I wouldn't like to see you get much bigger. Can you stand up?'

She struggled off the couch, and Leo stretched his long arms round her and circled her middle with the tape.

'Isn't this cosy?' he said with a chuckle, and Jenny smiled.

'It is rather a long way round, isn't it?'

'Hmm,' he said again, staring at the tape.

Jenny laughed. 'Are you trying to humiliate me into labour?' she asked him.

His mouth quirked. 'Not exactly. The average is about 101 cm — about 40 inches. Your "waist" measures 106 cm — so either you're well over your dates, you've been secretly bingeing, or you've got twins in there. Let's have a listen — hop back on the couch for me, could you?'

'I could only hear one,' Abbie said doubtfully, 'but perhaps I'm just not very good at listening?'

Leo chuckled and straightened up. 'I'm sure there's only one — if there are two, one of them's hiding very successfully. You've been scanned, haven't you?'

Jenny nodded. 'Yes, three months ago. They said it was a little on the small side, if anything.'

'Well, I think perhaps you should have another scan — tomorrow now, I think. I'll get our receptionist to ring the hospital and make you an appointment when Dr Pearce has finished with you, OK?'

She sighed in resignation. 'Yes, I suppose so.'

'Is that a problem?'

'Only that they make you drink gallons and then when you're dying for the loo they make you wait another ten minutes. I feel so distended at the moment anyway, the very thought of it makes me wince!'

Leo smiled sympathetically. 'Still, it's better to be on the safe side. If it is twins you really ought to be in hospital in plenty of time, and they'll want to induce you.'

She groaned. 'Oh, well, I'll go home and pack just in case,' she said with theatrical emphasis.

'Soon be over — did you do an internal?' he asked Abbie.

'Yes — there didn't seem to be any cervical change.'

'Hmm. OK, scan tomorrow, then, and we'll go from there.'

He left, the tape draped over his shoulder, whistling softly.

Jenny sighed. 'It's easy for him to be cheerful — he's never had a scan!'

'You'll be fine — I'll ring the hospital tomorrow for the result, OK?'

Jenny nodded and slipped her clothes back on while Abbie updated her file. She was the last patient, and Abbie had actually managed to finish her clinic by four for the first time.

Disgustingly pleased with herself, she wandered out into the office and was immediately accosted by Ravi.

'Oh, Abbie — I wonder if you'd do me the most enormous favour. . .?'

Abbie's heart sank. Ravi was on duty, and doing her a favour could mean only one thing.

'Tonight?' she said heavily.

'You're a darling — thank you so much. Richard's taking me out for dinner — it's his birthday and he thought he was on call, but he's managed to bribe one of his colleagues. You're a regular sweetheart.'

Only when it suits you, Abbie thought wearily. She really didn't want to be on duty that night — not that she had any definite arrangement with Leo, but they had fallen into the pattern of spending their evenings together when they weren't on call, and she had been looking forward to it. Still, it did free her on Thursday.

'Can you do Thursday for me?' she asked Ravinda as an afterthought.

'Thursday? Yes, of course — oh, no, I'm sorry, I forgot. I'm out again. Never mind; perhaps another time.'

She breezed off, leaving Abbie feeling deflated and used. Leo wandered in, took one look at her and asked what was wrong.

'Ravi—I'm covering for her tonight, but guess what? She's busy on Thursday.'

'Bitch,' he muttered, and a few minutes later she heard him tackling Ravi in her surgery.

She walked towards the door, ready to intervene, when she heard Ravi laugh.

'Oh, come on, Leo, lighten up. You can manage without sex for one night—and anyway, it won't hurt her to pull her weight. She's done damn all.'

'That's unfair, Ravi. She's worked very hard—she hasn't found it easy, and she's taken time to settle, I'll grant you, but she's improving every day——'

'Oh, come on, Leo! How long are you going to carry her? She's a passenger, and we can't afford passengers. Let her work two nights a week like the rest of us, and get an idea of what general practice is really like!'

'I will—when she's competent enough. At the moment, though, she lacks confidence and that could be dangerous. You need to be decisive——'

'Is that why she always calls on you for help? Because she's too scared to make her own decisions?'

'Because she's got enough sense to know when to ask,' he said furiously. 'And anyway, if I am carrying her, what's it to you? It's no skin off your nose, is it?'

'Except that you're tired, and so you perform badly. It won't be so bad if Colin comes back, but what if he doesn't? What if he has to retire early because of his back? We can't carry passengers when we're already one member of staff down—it isn't cost-effective, and it isn't fair either to us or to the patients. And if you weren't so obsessed with the inside of her pants you'd know that!'

Abbie turned blindly—and ran straight into Peter's chest. He must have heard it all, too.

'Oh, God, Abbie,' he said softly, and led her into his surgery, shutting the door firmly behind them.

She stared miserably up into his kind face. 'Am I a passenger, Peter? Is that how you feel about me?'

He shrugged his shoulders awkwardly. 'It's unfortunate that Colin's off at the same time. It's a busy practice, with lots of elderlies and also lots of young families, and there isn't a lot of slack. When the winter comes. . .' He shrugged eloquently. 'It can get very busy, and if we've got someone who isn't happy with the job, who needs spoon-feeding—well, it just adds to the stresses. I can see Ravi's point, but I can also see Leo's. You're beginning to shape up well. Who knows? With time you could be really good——'

'But just now this practice needs me like a hole in the head,' she finished for him. 'OK, Peter, I get the hint. Maybe it's just as well Colin's off and forcing the issue, because I can tell I'm not welcome here——'

'Oh, Abbie, that isn't so. You're very welcome. It's just that. . .'

Her mouth twisted into a sad little smile. 'Don't worry, Peter. I understand. I'll go.'

'No—no, Abbie, please. Wait and find out what's happening about Colin before you do anything hasty. After all, if we got anyone else it would take them time to settle in here——'

'But if you're a qualified GP with experience, you wouldn't need to worry about the clinical aspects of his or her work.'

Peter dropped his eyes. 'Abbie, please don't be hasty.'

She swallowed. 'OK, I won't. I'll wait until Colin has made a decision one way or the other, but if he's still off by Christmas I'll go anyway. OK?'

'Talk to Leo,' he urged.

'No. He knows how I feel about general practice. If he realises I overheard that conversation, he'll be mortified. He'll also try and talk me out of leaving out of guilt. No, Peter, leave it with me. I'll make a decision one way or the other, and then let you all know.'

He regarded her steadily for a moment, then gave her a swift hug.

'Attagirl. You'd better go and start your surgery or Ravi will complain you're taking too long again.'

'Why does she hate me?' Abbie asked, unable to keep the emotion out of her voice.

'She wanted Leo. He wasn't interested.'

'But she's got Richard now.'

'So?' Peter shrugged. 'You've still succeeded where she failed, and now she sees Leo helping you out when he's always been the one to criticise her in the past for inefficiency. I guess it just galls her. I don't suppose it's really personal.'

'Well, it damn well feels it,' Abbie confided.

Peter patted her shoulder and opened the door. 'Don't worry about her. Just go and do your surgery and forget about all of this.'

She shot him a grateful smile. 'Thanks.'

'My pleasure.'

She got through her surgery somehow, and then the after-surgery visits, which were thankfully straight-forward. She would have died before she'd call Leo for advice.

Unfortunately the situation deteriorated shortly after midnight.

Jenny Dobson's husband rang, almost hysterical, to say that she had woken in labour and was already pushing.

'I'll be right with you,' Abbie told him.

She dressed in seconds, but before she left the flat she rang Leo.

'Jenny Dobson's in labour—I didn't think I should go it alone,' she told him crisply, and put the phone down without waiting for a reply.

Then she ran downstairs, banged the door behind her and jumped in her car, heading off towards the outskirts of town. She knew where they lived, as Leo had pointed it out to her in the past, and it took her only five minutes to get there.

Leo, however, was there before her, to her great relief. The front door was open and she went in and called.

'Up here,' a man's voice said, and she ran up the stairs and found Jenny in bed, propped up against the pillows.

'Baby's crowning,' Leo said tersely. 'Got a maternity pack handy?'

She had, in her hand, and quickly opened it and spread out the contents.

'Can I wash my hands?' she asked the husband, and he directed her to the bathroom next door.

She was just drying them when there was a wail, and Leo laughed. She ran back in to find him cradling the baby's head in his hands.

'Here we go! Lusty lungs—one more gentle push, Jenny—that's lovely—well done.'

The baby slithered into the world with another yell, and Leo grinned and laid him over his mother's thigh.

'Well, young man, that was a bit precipitate, wasn't it? Can you make a note of the time, Abbie?'

Jenny was laughing, her husband was beaming in relief, but Leo suddenly went very still.

'Jenny — can you push again for me, my love? Very gently? That's lovely — and again.'

Abbie stared in astonishment as another tiny head appeared, damp curls clustered against the purple skin, and a second baby slipped into Leo's hands. It was another boy, and for an awful moment Abbie thought the baby was lifeless.

Then Leo flicked his feet and he yanked up his knees, screwed up his face and bawled his indignation.

'My God, it *was* twins,' Leo said in awe, and turned to Abbie. 'The scan?'

'One must have been masked.' She bent over the babies and grinned. 'They're lovely — noisy, but wonderful. Congratulations!'

Jenny's eyes filled up, and she gazed down in wonder at her new little family. 'They're just — so perfect. . .'

The tears slipped down her cheeks, and her husband climbed on to the other side of the bed, put one arm round her shoulders and hugged her. 'Well done, love,' he said unevenly, and she turned and kissed him.

'Two.'

'Double trouble.'

They hugged each other, and Leo turned to Abbie and smiled in satisfaction.

'Saves going through it all twice, I suppose,' he said cheerfully. 'Now, little chaps, we ought to get you cleaned up and back to your mum. Would you like to

take over? This should have been your delivery,' he
said to Abbie.

She nodded, wondering whether he had carried on
after she arrived because there was no time to do
anything else, or because he didn't trust her.

She would never know, she realised, and she put the
clips on the cords and cut them very thoughtfully.

The placenta came away quite spontaneously, and as
there was only one it proved that the twins were
identical.

She weighed them, noting that they were a very
respectable weight, both over 2.8 kilos, and then she
washed them one at a time and handed them back to
the mother.

'Did you ring the midwife?' she asked Mr Dobson.

'Yes—she was out on another call. Her husband
suggested ringing you.'

She nodded. Just so long as she knew. She didn't
want to tread on anybody else's toes.

The babies were lovely, quite perfect, no clicky hips
or funny heart noises that she could detect—although
that could be because she had missed them.

'Are you OK?' Leo asked her softly.

'Mmm. Just sentimental. Babies do that to me,' she
told him. It wasn't an outright lie, just perhaps a little
economical with the truth.

She poured away the bath-water and rinsed out the
bath, then went back into the bedroom to find Leo
trying to persuade the babies to drink.

'Are you any good at this, Abbie?' he asked her.

'It's a knack,' she told him.

'I know—I don't have it.'

She laughed. 'Move over, then. Right, young

man——' She grasped the baby's head, brushed his cheek against the nipple and as he turned, mouth open, she pushed his head hard against the breast. He started to suckle immediately.

'Now for your brother. Here we go—there. Easy as falling off a log.'

Jenny's face was glazed with happiness, and her husband was bursting with pride, dashing round the bed with a camera trying to get the best shots.

After a few minutes the babies dozed off, and Leo suggested having a look to see if Jenny needed any repairs.

'Just a couple of stiches—do you want to do them, Dr Pearce?'

Her confidence, restored by the breast-feeding episode, slumped again.

'If you like,' she said diffidently.

He stood up and thankfully moved away, so that he wasn't standing over her watching her make a mockery of the woman's perineum. In fact the stiches were easy ones, and she had no trouble at all. She had tackled much worse ones in her time on maternity.

'There—all perfect again. Wash them several times a day in salty water to keep the skin clean, and they can come out in six or seven days. The midwife will keep an eye on them for you.'

She thought Leo had gone, but he was waiting for her in the hall below, talking to Mr Dobson.

As she walked out she overheard another conversation she would rather have missed.

Mr Dobson was thanking Leo for coming out, and saying how glad he was in view of the fact that Abbie was only training.

'She's a fully qualified doctor,' Leo replied. 'She's with us for a year deciding whether she wants to be a GP. In a hospital she'd be a registrar by now, and quite senior. I don't think you need have any fears about her professional competence.'

'Oh, I didn't realise. Well, I'm still glad you were able to come. Experience counts for a lot, and we've waited such a long time.'

Abbie went into the bathroom, flushed the loo and came out noisily on to the landing. 'Right, I'm off now,' she said louder than was necessary. 'I'll pop back and see you tomorrow.'

She went downstairs, gave Mr Dobson a professional and—she hoped—normal smile, and bade him goodnight.

'Goodnight, Dr Chandler,' she said to Leo, and walked past him without a glance.

He followed her out. 'Want to come back for a drink?' he asked softly.

'I don't think so. I wouldn't like to keep you up any longer.'

She turned away, but he turned her back. 'What is it, Abbie?'

She debated for a second, but then decided on the truth. 'I'm just sick to death of everyone doubting my professional competence—me included. Now, if you don't mind, I'd like to go home.'

She turned away again, and this time he let her go. She glanced up in the rear-view mirror, and in the light from the porch she could see that he was still watching her, his face thoughtful.

CHAPTER NINE

THE thump on her door shortly after she arrived home
didn't surprise Abbie. She let him in, simply because
she knew he would knock the door down before he
gave up and went away.

'Do you want to talk about it?' he asked.

'Not especially,' she told him bitterly. 'I should have
thought there was very little to add.'

'You overheard Dobson saying he was glad I was
there.'

'That's right.' She didn't mention Ravi—it was complicated enough.

'Did you also hear him say how highly Jenny spoke
of you, and how she was desperate that you should be
the one to deliver her?'

Abbie blinked. 'She said that?'

'Yes—apparently. Ask her, don't take my word for
it. I only did it because I was sitting there on the bed
between her feet and the damn babies just came out!
What could I do? You were still washing your hands.
It's a good job I live as close as I do or her husband
would have been doing it.'

Her shoulders drooped with relief. 'I thought you
didn't trust me to do it,' she confided.

'Oh, Abbie—I know obstetrics is one of your fortes.
I would have been quite happy to let you do the whole
thing.'

'I wasn't,' she told him quietly. 'I was so relieved you were there.'

'You would have coped.'

'As it happened, yes. But what if something had gone wrong?'

He pulled her against his chest. 'You would have been just as scared as any of the rest of us, and just as likely to do the right thing.'

She sighed shakily. 'I don't think so.'

'You should. Come on; I must go, and you ought to be in bed. The phone could ring at any time.'

She grabbed his hand. 'Leo?'

He paused, looking down at her.

'Stay the night.'

'I can't, you know that.'

'At least for a while — please?'

He searched her face, and then finally sighed. 'OK — just for a while, but I must go before the morning. Can't have you compromised.'

His grin was crooked and appealing. Abbie leant against him with a sigh.

If only she were more confident.

If only he loved her.

If only he would admit it.

If only life were much less complicated instead of bristling with if onlys.

'Come on, bed,' he said gently, and ushered her into her room.

They didn't make love, simply lay together, his arms round her, her head pillowed on his chest while she listened to the steady beat of his heart beneath her ear and wished she had the power to change things.

When the phone rang she answered it groggily, then

swung her legs over the side and stood up. She had learned long ago that unless she did that she went back to sleep. While she listened, she tugged on her clothes.

Leo propped himself up on one elbow. 'Going out?' he mouthed.

She nodded, jotting down the address, then cradled the phone.

'It's an elderly man I've never seen, with chest pain. I may be some time.'

He nodded. 'I should admit him if you're doubtful.' He swung his legs over the side and stood up, walking unselfconsciously towards her, folding her into his arms for a brief hug. 'You'll be fine. Go on.'

She went. The man, in his late eighties, was clearly very ill and unlikely to make it through the night. She admitted him and went home, unsurprised to find Leo gone.

The bed was still warm, though, and the sheets carried the faint scent of his body. She snuggled closer, and within seconds she was asleep.

There were no more calls that night, and Abbie went into work on the Tuesday morning feeling surprisingly able to cope.

One of her visits after morning surgery was to the widow of the man she had been called out to in the night. She was still a little shocked, and Abbie had a cup of tea with her and talked it through before leaving. On the way back to the surgery she popped in to see the Dobson twins, and found them all well. The midwife had been and declared her stitching excellent, apparently, and that bolstered Abbie's ego further.

Then she got back to the surgery to find that the nurse counsellor from the hospice had rung to say that she was concerned about Clare Tanner, who was complaining of chest pain. Could Abbie see her?

Her confidence deserted her, and she went straight in to find Leo.

He was just signing a stack of scrips, and turned to her with a grin.

'How are the babies?'

'Fine. How did you know I'd been to see them?'

'Intuition.' The grin widened. 'I knew you couldn't resist it. What's the problem?'

She told him about Clare.

'So what particularly worries you about seeing her?'

She shrugged. 'I've had no real training in bereavement counselling, and I'm so scared I'll say the wrong thing.'

'You think this pain is related to her mother's death?'

'I'm almost sure of it — and if it is, what do I say?'

Leo reached behind him and pulled a book off the shelves. 'Here — how to talk to people who are dying, or have relatives who are dying or have died. It's very useful. When are you seeing her?'

She looked at the book. It was only fairly slim, but she wanted to read it carefully.

'I don't know — tomorrow?'

He nodded. 'Look, I'm busy now, but let's have a role-play session on this later — after surgery? Then we can go on and have a meal somewhere. Peter's on call tonight.'

She nodded. 'Thanks — I'd appreciate it.'

His eyebrows shot up. 'Wonders will never cease.'

She gave a hollow laugh. 'Perhaps I've never been sufficiently desperate before. I'll go and start reading this now before my surgery.'

She skimmed the book, dipping into areas which looked as if they might be useful, and promising herself further reading later.

Her surgery was mercifully short, and she was able to get through her patients with an efficiency that surprised her.

It also surprised Jackie, the receptionist.

'You're finished early — if you go on like this I'll have to give you more patients.'

Abbie glanced into the waiting-room. There were still two people sitting there.

'Who are they for?'

'Leo — but then he had five more than you.'

Abbie's brow creased in a frown. 'Why?'

She shrugged. 'He always does. They all do. Well, you take longer. It saves the patients waiting time.'

'But that isn't fair,' Abbie said quietly. 'Why should the others carry my workload?'

She shrugged again. 'Search me — Leo's idea. They've been doing it since the end of your second week.'

Abbie stared at her, then took a deep breath. 'Well, it's not happening any more. In future I'll see my fair share, whatever Leo says.'

'Well, you'd better clear it with him. I value my job!'

'No — say nothing. Just do it, Jackie — please? I'm sick of everybody grudgingly making allowances for me. It isn't necessary, and I resent it.'

She saw respect dawn in Jackie's eyes. 'OK — but don't let me down by taking ages and leaving them hanging about, or Leo'll kill me.'

'I'll defend you,' Abbie said drily, and, finding

herself a cup of coffee, she curled up in the staffroom
with the book.

A few minutes later Leo came in. 'Oh, you're done.'

'Yes. Your place or mine?'

'Can we do it at the cottage? I have to feed the damn
cat.'

She stifled a smile. 'Fine. Let me get my stuff and
I'll follow you there.'

She arrived at the cottage to find Tiger standing on
the worktop yowling, his nose in danger of being
amputated by the can opener as he watched Leo
struggle with the lid.

'Demanding little blighter,' Leo grumbled as he
tipped the food out into a dish and plonked both it and
the cat on to the floor. 'Right, let's have a drink and
talk about Clare.'

They settled down at the table.

'OK,' Leo said, 'now imagine I'm Clare, and I come
in and tell you I've got this pain in my chest, and I feel
sick. What are you going to ask her?'

Abbie shrugged. 'Does she feel sick only when she
has the pain, or all the time, or aren't they related.
Also where is the pain?'

He nodded. 'OK, but not too much at once. Remember she's only twelve, and not likely to be concentrating
too much on what you're saying but on what she's
saying. You need to concentrate on that, too. Look for
what she's leaving out. Watch her body—is she awkward, tense, slumped? Does she look depressed? Or is
she over-bright? If you don't get any joy, ask her how
Josephine and her father are coping. That may tell you
a lot, because I suspect she feels she needs to be strong

for them, to take over from her mother, and the strain is just too much.'

'I can imagine it would be. Poor little girl.'

'Try sympathy. Look all the time for a chink in her armour, and see if you can get her to cry. I suspect all that's wrong is that she's bottled up all her feelings and is terrified to let them out. I know the nurse at St Saviour is getting absolutely nowhere with her, although Jo is doing really very well.'

'How's Gerry?'

'Devastated, but coming through the stages well. He started his grieving nearly two months before she died, so he's well on the way to acceptance now, although he's still very sad and misses her desperately. He will, of course, for years, but at least the psychological progress of grief is proceeding along the proper course.'

Abbie nodded. 'Yes, I think Clare could well be arrested in the denial phase.'

'OK. Let's run through a few possibilities. I'll be Clare, you be you and we'll see how you might go about tackling the consultation.'

They worked on it for nearly two hours, then Leo called a halt.

'Fine. I think you've got that pretty well sorted out. I don't think there's anything we've left out that's of major importance, but, just in case, make the appointment with her for when I'm around, and nip out and ask me anything you aren't sure of. Don't phone — you can be more frank if she can't hear you. OK?'

She nodded. 'Thanks, I'm sure that will help.'

'I can't get over all this gratitude,' he teased. 'Are you going to express it in the the time-honoured fashion, or do you want to eat first?'

She grinned. 'I'd love to oblige, but I'm likely to faint if I don't eat something soon. Do we have to go out?'

'No, but I haven't got anything exciting — cat food, baked beans and a few potatoes — oh, and a bit of cheese. I desperately need to go shopping.'

'How about a take-away?'

'Kebabs?'

'Mmm — lovely.'

'Can you stand the lecture on the quality of English lamb and the paucity of decent salad ingredients?'

She chuckled. 'I'll tough it out.'

'Poor Spiro. I think he's secretly homesick.'

'Well, I hope he doesn't go back — his kebabs are fantastic!'

'Tell him that. He needs his ego bolstering.'

Don't we all? she thought, sobering, and wondered how she would cope with Clare the next day.

The child looked awful — thin, drawn, her eyes vacant. Even expecting her to be unhappy, Abbie was shocked. She smiled and patted the chair beside her desk.

'Come and sit down and have a chat. I gather you don't feel very well,' she said casually.

'No. I've got this pain — sort of here.' The girl indicated the region over her heart.

Abbie busied herself taking Clare's pulse and blood-pressure, anxious to check for any real physical symptoms just to be on the safe side.

'Does the pain come and go, or is it there all the time?' she asked.

'Mostly all the time. Sometimes it's worse.'

'Any particular time?'

Abbie was watching her carefully as she asked the casual question, and noticed the tension creep into the girl's shoulders.

'No, not really.'

Abbie changed tack. 'How are your father and sister coping?'

The tension increased. 'All right,' she said shortly.

'It must be very sad for you all at home at the moment — I expect you're having to do a lot to help.'

'I don't mind,' she said, too quickly.

'Don't you? I'm sure I would. You're very young to have to take over the responsibility for your sister and father.'

'I don't mind,' she repeated emphatically. 'I feel sick, too, sometimes.'

Abbie noticed the deliberate change of subject. So, she was close to the truth.

'You know,' she said quietly, 'even the strong ones need to lean on someone some of the time. Otherwise they get ill. Pains like this often mean people are under pressure, and there's no physical cause for the pain at all——'

'I'm not inventing it!' Clare said desperately. 'I do feel sick, and I have got a pain!'

'I'm sure you have,' Abbie told her gently. 'It's called heartache. You must be terribly sad now your mother's dead.'

Clare's hands flew up over her ears. 'Don't say that!' she cried.

'But it's true — and it's hurting you very badly, isn't it?'

'No!' she whispered, her eyes wide and empty, and

then suddenly she began to shake. 'No, no, please, no. . .'

Abbie wrapped her arms round the slender shoulders and let Clare cry, hugely relieved that the dam was at least breached, if not completely broken. She could feel the tension in her still, the fighting against her feelings, and she smoothed her hair down and rocked her.

'There, there — it's all right to cry. It'll make you stronger. It's all right, I've got you; you're quite safe.'

The crying increased, and Abbie felt the tension draining slowly from the heaving shoulders until the girl lay against her, hiccuping occasionally. Her hands were clinging to Abbie's jumper, and her face was buried in her lap.

Abbie let her lie there until the shudders stopped, and then helped her sit up and gave her a tissue.

'Do you want to talk about it?'

Clare nodded. 'It's awful at home now. Jo cries all the time, and I have to comfort her, and I shouldn't. Mum should be there to do it.'

'Does it make you angry that she isn't?'

Clare nodded, surprised. 'Yes — very angry. I'm not ready to be without her.'

'No, I don't suppose you are — any of you. You all loved her very much, didn't you? That's why it hurts so badly.'

Clare nodded again. 'Dad cries at night. I hear him in his room, and it's all muffled as if he's got his head under the pillows but I can still hear, even if I put my head under my pillows. It's awful, it goes on and on, and then in the morning he gets up and his eyes are all red and he tries to smile but he can't ——'

She broke off, her face contorted, and bit her lip. 'I knew it would be hard, but — I'm so lonely without her. . .'

The tears slid down her cheeks but this time she sat there and let them fall, talking through them as if now she had started she didn't know how to stop.

Abbie listened, putting in the odd comment or question to keep her going, and after a while she ground to a halt, clearly exhausted.

'I think you've had enough for now, don't you?' Abbie said gently.

Clare nodded and sniffed. 'Mmm. Thanks for listening. I feel much better.'

Abbie smiled. 'My pleasure. How's the pain?'

She looked surprised. 'It's nearly gone.'

'Good. It will go, gradually. Don't worry. Come and talk to me again, whenever you like. I'm always around. OK? Here, I'll give you my number at the flat — you might find me there in the evening if you're desperate.'

'Don't you mind?'

Abbie shook her head. 'No — truly, I don't mind at all. It's good to be able to help you.'

Clare gave her a watery smile. 'Mum liked you. She said you were kind and sensible. She was right.'

Abbie's eyes filled up. 'Thank you, Clare,' she said unsteadily. 'Thank you very much.'

She hugged Clare briefly, and then showed her out to the waiting-room where Gerry was in conversation with Leo. They turned, and Gerry held out his arms to Clare, who walked into them and gave him a huge hug.

'Hi — can we go home now?'

Gerry met Abbie's eyes over her head. She smiled. 'She's fine — a bit sad, but she'll be OK.'

Gerry nodded. 'Thanks.'

'My pleasure.'

They left, and Leo turned to Abbie.

'So, how was it?'

'Draining. Can we go for a drink? I need one.'

'I'm on duty.'

'Damn. Your place? I just need to unwind.'

'Sure — but bring your car. You'll need it to get home if I'm called out.'

They left, and sure enough he was called out almost immediately.

Abbie sat in front of the television, Tiger turning her knee into a pin-cushion, and sipped her way through a glass of wine. The phone rang again, and she answered it.

'Sorry, he's out. Try him on the mobile — have you got the number?'

'Oh — it's urgent. It's my husband — I think he's tried to kill himself.'

Abbie recognised the voice. 'Mrs Clarke?'

'Yes — is that Dr Pearce?'

'Yes, it is. What makes you think he's tried suicide?'

'He's in the garage — I found him with the door shut and the engine running, but the garage door's got an automatic closer on it so it might have shut when he drove in and then he could have forgotten to turn the engine off.'

'Have you turned it off now and opened the door?'

'Yes — and dragged him out into the garden, but he's still unconscious and I think he's dying.'

'Don't worry, I'll come myself. Stay with him. I'll call an ambulance and I'll be with you.'

She rang ambulance control, gave them the address and ran outside after scribbling a note for Leo. It took her ten minutes to get to the Clarkes' house, and she found Mrs Clarke crouched on the gravel drive beside the recumbent form of her husband.

Abbie jumped out of her car and ran over to them, kneeling down in the gravel and laying her head against his chest. He was alive but still unconscious, and in the glare from the security lights on the front of the house she could see he was very pale, and there was a bluish tinge around his lips.

'I'll give him some oxygen,' she said briefly, and found the portable oxygen cylinder and mask in the boot of her car. All of the doctors in the practice carried one as a matter of routine, and for weeks it had driven Abbie mad clunking about in the boot. Now, however, she was profoundly grateful for it.

She had just attached the mask to his face when Leo turned up. She heard the car door slam and the crunch of gravel, then he was beside her, hunkering down and doing a quick verbal check with her while his eyes and hands were busy running over the patient.

They heard the siren on the ambulance, then the van was backing up and the ambulance men were loading him up and taking him away as soon as Leo had scribbled a quick letter for the medical reg on take.

Mrs Clarke went with them, and Leo checked that the house was locked before they could go back to the cottage.

'What about Maxie?' Abbie asked, puzzled.

'She's at boarding-school—just started this term.

She's getting on really well, apparently. It's for musically gifted autistic children, and it suits her down to the ground. Suits the Clarkes as well, I should think.'

'Do you suppose he tried to top himself?' Abbie asked thoughtfully.

'No—I think he probably had an MI on the way home. He's been seeing me for chest pain in the past few weeks, and we've done an ECG. It was OK but it showed a silent infarct some time in the recent past. He was booked for investigation by the cardiac specialist.'

'Well, he's certainly jumped up the queue now,' Abbie said.

'Hmm. Thanks for coming out—I owe you.'

She grinned. 'Consider us quits for the training session the other night.'

'I thought you'd already paid for that,' he said softly.

'So I did. Oh, well. . .'

He slipped an arm round her shoulders. 'You could always come back to my place.'

'For what? Some coitus interruptus? You're on call.'

He gave a rueful grin. 'Oh, well—tomorrow?

'I'm on call myself.'

He sighed. 'Friday?'

'Sure—if I can stay awake.'

His smile flashed in the dark. 'I'll see to it that you can.' He kissed her briefly. 'See you tomorrow, then—and thanks again for tonight.'

She watched as he drove away, then turned her car and headed home.

The flat had never seemed so empty as it did that night. She wondered if she was crazy to continue her relationship with him, when all he wanted from her was an affair, pure and simple.

No commitment, no strings — certainly no opportunity to dig herself into his life and make herself indispensable.

She couldn't walk away from him, though — not while she saw him every day. There was only one cure, one solution, and that was to move away, but she didn't have the strength.

As for a career in general practice, she was still most unsure about the diversity of ailments she would have to deal with and her ability to do so. One idea, though, had formed in her mind over the past few weeks. Something she would never have thought of until recently.

She would leave it to the gods. If Colin returned to work, she would stay. If, however, he was unable to, and they had to relocate her for the remainder of her training, she would give up her GP aspirations and follow this other path.

Now all she had to do was sit back and wait.

CHAPTER TEN

IN FACT it was the beginning of November, more than three weeks later, before Abbie's decision was made for her.

Colin Williams, the senior partner, came into the surgery for the Monday morning practice meeting and very solemnly and sadly gave them the news that he had decided to take early retirement.

'I'm sorry, I know it's all a bit sudden, but I just feel I won't be able to pull my weight and I won't do myself any favours, either, if I stay. Megan and I have a lot of things we'd like to do, and so it seems fortuitous, in a way, that this has happened.'

Fortuitous, or just another kick of fate? Abbie wondered. Now the decision was made and the time had come, how did she really feel? Numb, she decided.

Colin carried on, confirming what she already knew.

'However fortuitous for me, it does, however, leave Abbie in a difficult position, because as the only qualified trainer in the practice I'm the only one able to oversee her traineeship officially. Not, I'm sure, that Leo hasn't done an excellent job, but unfortunately his sterling work isn't counted.'

He met Abbie's eyes. 'So I'm afraid, my dear, that we're both out in the cold. I do apologise. I'm sure that you'll be able to find another practice fairly soon without any trouble.'

She dredged up a smile. 'Please don't worry. I've

been thinking for some time that general practice wasn't my niche in life. You've just helped me crystallise my thoughts into a decision.'

She looked round at them all; Peter, who had become a friend and ally; Ravi, who was probably only being honest but whose words had hurt more than Abbie could say; Peggy, the practice manager, who had supported her even at her most inefficient; Jackie, the receptionist, who had teased her about the PC4s; and Leo — Leo whom she loved to distraction, whose absence in her life would rob it of all meaning, but whose presence turned it into a painful farce.

His face was a mask, registering no emotion, no flicker of what he was really thinking. Had she ever known?

'Abbie, are you sure?' Peter asked.

'Yes — yes, I'm sure. Ravi's right,' she continued quietly. 'I've been a passenger — not because I haven't wanted to pull my weight, but because I've been unable to. You've all had to carry me, and I'm sorry. I didn't mean to be a burden. Perhaps when I've gone you'll be able to get someone part-time who will be more cost-effective than I am and achieve probably a great deal more.'

She flashed Ravi a little smile and was surprised to see remorse on her usually enigmatic features.

'How did you know?' the woman asked hesitantly.

Abbie's smile faltered at the remembered pain. 'I overheard you talking to Leo a few weeks ago. Anyway, whatever. . .it doesn't matter. I've learned a lot here — perhaps the most important lesson being that I need to be involved — deeply involved — with what I'm doing. General practice is too fragmented, too unpredictable for me. I can't cope with it, and I find it unfulfilling and unsettling. I suppose it would be different in a single-handed practice, but I certainly couldn't cope with that.'

She paused, and Leo's voice cut into the silence. 'So what will you do?'

She couldn't look at him. 'Terminal care.'

'What?' Leo exclaimed. 'But you hate it—it tears you to pieces!'

'No, it hurts me—but at the same time it gives my life some purpose.' She took a deep breath and rushed on, 'Working with Mary Tanner was the nearest I've ever come to being of some real use. I know I couldn't change the course of her illness, but with your guidance, and by listening and understanding, I hope I was able to make the outcome more acceptable for her and for her family.'

Leo nodded. 'Yes, you did. She appreciated your input very much.'

'I've also spent a great deal of time with her daughters in the past couple of weeks, and that's helped me to realise that I really want to specialise in that area of medicine.' She lifted her hands. 'So there you have it— my *raison d'être*.'

A stunned silence followed her announcement, and then Colin drew everyone's attention back to the arrangements that would need to be made to appoint his successor.

Abbie paid little attention. It was all irrelevant to her anyway—except the bit about her being freed from her contract as soon as a suitable locum could be found to cover for Colin.

She made her escape immediately the meeting

closed, starting her surgery promptly and rattling through her patients with unprecedented efficiency.

As the last one left, so Ravi slipped through the door.

'Abbie?'

She shut down her computer and looked at the woman whose words had hurt her so badly. 'What can I do for you, Ravi?'

'It's what I can do for you — if it's not too late. I wanted to apologise. That argument you overheard — it wasn't meant for your ears. I was just jealous of you — silly, I know, because I'd already met Richard and things were going well, but Leo and I — well, let's just say I would have liked things to have gone differently, and I hated you for succeeding where I had failed. Anyway, I was just using you as a way of having a go at him ——'

'Hence the remark about being obsessed with the inside of my pants?'

Even under her dusky skin Abbie could see the woman blush. 'I'm sorry; that was incredibly vulgar and uncalled for. As I said, I was jealous — not only of the time he spent with you in private, but the time he spent with you in the surgery, helping you out with the patients and the computer and the routine, dragging you here, there and everywhere, spoon-feeding you almost. When I started here two years ago I wasn't allowed any mistakes — he was quite ruthless. It hurt to see him being so lenient with you.'

'But you were right,' Abbie argued. 'I was carried by all of you for a long while, and that wasn't strictly fair.'

Ravi shrugged. 'It was Colin's absence that was the

real problem, not your presence. And in fact you've done a good job now you've settled in. I'm just so sorry you had to overhear that particular conversation.'

Abbie smiled ruefully. 'It hurt, but it wouldn't have made any difference. I'm not a natural GP, Ravi. It just helped me to make up my mind. I suppose I should be grateful to you.'

She stacked the notes on her desk, hoping the woman would go away and leave her to organise her thoughts as well as her paperwork.

'What about Leo?' Ravi asked softly.

Abbie froze. 'What about Leo?'

'Oh, dear. I'm sorry, Abbie.'

She swallowed. 'Yes, well, you win some, you lose some. I knew at the beginning it was a risk.'

'I'm still sorry.'

The door closed softly, and Abbie folded her arms and laid her head on them.

It hurt.

It shouldn't have surprised her, but it did. She thought she was ready, thought she'd made the decision to leave if Colin resigned, but theory and practice were clearly different things.

And it hurt so damn much!

She bit her lip. She still had to face Leo — and she had a feeling that that interview would be horribly difficult.

Please, God, let her be able to put it off as long as possible.

She managed to avoid him till lunchtime, then he cornered her in the office.

'That was a bit sudden, wasn't it?'

'No. Do you want a coffee?'

'No, I don't want a bloody coffee, I want an explanation. You were coming on really well, making a lot of progress. Why give up now?'

She forced herself to look at him at last.

'Why not?' she asked quietly. 'It isn't me, Leo. OK, so with practice I'm managing to make less of a mess of it, but I still don't like it; I still find myself running on adrenalin and I can't live like that.'

'It gets better, Abbie. With time and experience you'd find it all much easier ——'

'But it isn't what I want to do! I want to work in terminal care, Leo — somewhere like St Saviour. I feel as if I matter there, as if I can make a difference. Mary Tanner taught me another lesson. Life's too short to waste it doing something that makes you unhappy if it's in your power to change it.'

He took her shoulders in his hands and drew her closer. 'Have you really been so unhappy here?' he asked softly.

She looked up into his eyes. Was it just wishful thinking on her part, or did he look as if he really cared whether she left or not? She looked away, none the wiser.

'Yes, I have.'

'Oh, Abbie, I'm sorry,' he murmured, and drew her gently into his arms. 'I'll kill Ravi for saying all that.'

Abbie sighed. 'It isn't Ravi. She's apologised already.' It's you, she wanted to add. If you would only admit you love me, things could be so different — not professionally, but personally, for me — you would fulfil me, she wanted to say, but instead she turned her face into his shoulder and bit her lip. It was pointless pleading with him. She knew the rules.

After a moment he spoke again. 'Peggy's rung the recruitment agency we use, and they've got a man who's just moved down from the Midlands to be nearer to his wife's family. At the moment he's still working in Solihull and commuting at the weekend, but it looks as though the practice would be right up his street. He's got the equity, and he's a trainer, too, so if he came you could finish your year—if you wanted to.'

For a moment she was tempted, standing here in his arms, the warmth of his skin under her hands through the fine cotton of his shirt, the slight scent of his skin teasing her senses—how easy it would be to let it drift, to stay and carry on her fruitless affair. Maybe even with time he might admit that he cared—but if not, what then? Would she have to work beside him day after day, perhaps watching him with another woman?

The shaft of pain that went through her took her breath away.

No, she had to leave, to get right away from him. She would never forget him but, in time, perhaps the pain would lessen and she would be able to rebuild her life.

She eased away from him. 'I don't think so, Leo.'

'Leo, call for you—Mrs Clarke,' Peggy called through the door, and with a muffled curse he left the room.

Abbie sagged against the table, her legs suddenly shaking. Please, God, let this man want to come soon, so that she could get away. Now the decision was made, every day would be agony.

* * *

In fact her pain was to be very short-lived, because the man had come to the end of his time in Solihull, the new partner had taken over and he was available immediately. He had decided to take a few weeks off and have a holiday, but in the circumstances he agreed to start the following Monday.

Abbie, who had wanted him there as soon as possible, now found herself wishing he could break his ankle and put off the evil day.

She rang her brother Tom, who lived in Cambridge.

'Come and help me move out of my flat this weekend,' she told him.

He asked no questions—Abbie knew he would save them for later.

She was rostered for duty on the Tuesday and Friday nights, and refused to change. 'I'll do my bit,' she told them.

Leo was on duty on Monday and Thursday, which left only Wednesday.

'Let me take you out for dinner,' Leo suggested on Wednesday morning.

'No, I'm too tired,' she said, and she was—tired of hiding her emotions, tired of pretending that all was well and that every time he took her in his arms her heart didn't break a little further. She couldn't stand a romantic, candlelit goodbye.

'When are you leaving?' he asked then.

'Saturday morning.'

'Saturday? But then tonight's our last chance,' he protested.

'Yes.'

He stared at her, bewildered, no doubt, that she could turn down the opportunity to enjoy his lovemaking one last time. 'Give my love to the cat,' she said, and went back into her surgery, calling the first patient before Leo had a chance to follow her.

The rest of the week was an emotional see-saw for Abbie. Many of the patients seemed genuinely sorry to see her go. She paid one last visit to the Dobson twins, bumped into Mrs Clarke outside the shops and dis-covered that her husband was improving after his heart attack and near-fatal accident with the exhaust fumes, and went for supper with the Tanners on the Thursday. They were coping well, considering, and were all very sorry to see her go.

She bade them a tearful goodbye, and went back to her flat to start packing.

On Friday evening her brother arrived, and she let him in on her way out on a call. She got back to find she had had a visitor.

'Big chap, fair hair—he looked furious when I opened the door. I told him you'd be back later.'

'Leo,' she said with a sigh. 'Oh, damn. I thought I'd got away with it.'

'Care to explain?'

'Not really. Make me a cup of tea, there's a good chap, and don't ask questions. I don't feel up to it just now. Get the phone; I'm having a bath.'

The doorbell rang again just as she lowered herself into the water. She heard voices, then the front door banged and her brother ran back upstairs.

'Leo again,' he told her through the door. 'I told him you were in the bath—I thought he was going to hit me.'

'Did you say who you were?'

'No.'

'Oh, dear,' Abbie said with a sigh. 'Oh, well, do him good to get jealous. It will be a salutary experience, I have no doubt.'

She dried herself slowly — her face more than once, because it kept getting wet again despite all her efforts — and then she dressed in fresh clothes and went into the little sitting-room, staring round in despair at the heaps of boxes.

'How can I have accumulated so much junk in three and a half months?' she asked in amazement.

Tom chuckled. 'You always were a squirrel.' His voice softened, filled with concern. 'Abbie, what is it?'

'What's what?'

'Oh, come on. You look like hell.'

'Thanks. You always were good for my ego.'

'Tell your big bro.'

She shook her head. 'No — sorry, Tom, I can't. It's all too fresh.'

'You're not pregnant?' he demanded indignantly.

'Oh, don't be so bloody melodramatic. No, I'm not pregnant.'

'That's all right, then.'

Abbie could have hit him. It was far from all right. At least if she'd been pregnant she would have had something of Leo to take with her, some part of him to keep——

The tears fell, refusing to co-operate, and she found herself cradled against a big, hard chest that reminded her painfully of Leo's. The tears fell even faster, and Tom patted her awkwardly.

The phone rang.

'Oh, hell,' she muttered, and pushed away from him

to answer it. When she put the phone down Tom was watching her expectantly.

'Well?'

'He's a bachelor, OK? That's all there is to it.'

Understanding dawned on Tom's face. 'Oh, sis — how could you fall for that line?'

She sniffed and glared at him. 'What do you mean, how could I fall for that line? The line you've been putting about for nigh on fifteen years?'

He shifted awkwardly. 'I've just never met the right girl.'

'Well, obviously Leo hasn't either. Now if you'll excuse me I want to make myself respectable before I go out on this call.'

She pushed past him into the bathroom, repaired the damage to her face and went out.

It was a hectic night — general practice getting its pound of flesh, she thought wryly as she went out for the fifth time shortly before seven the following morning.

She arrived back to find Leo's car outside and Tom stacking boxes on the pavement.

'He's back,' Tom said unnecessarily. 'Wouldn't leave without speaking to you.'

Abbie sighed. 'Oh, hell. Look amuse yourself for a while, could you? I'd better see him.'

She went slowly up the stairs, her heart pounding. She hated goodbyes in the best of circumstances, and these hardly qualified.

He was standing at the window. 'Who is that?' he asked tightly.

'Tom? My brother.'

His shoulders dropped an inch. 'I thought. . .'

'What? That I'd replaced you already? What a blow to your ego.'

She hated herself for the sarcastic tone of her voice, but she couldn't help it; watching him standing there, the pain was overwhelming.

'I wanted to talk to you before you left.'

'So I gathered.'

He looked awkward, curiously vulnerable, and Abbie's hopes lifted.

'There's a case I want to put to you,' he began, and her heart sank again.

'A thirty-two-year-old professional man?' she said drily.

His mouth quirked slightly. 'You guessed.'

Her temper, stressed beyond endurance by the strain of their abortive relationship, finally snapped.

'Leo, for God's sake, grow up!' she retaliated. 'For months you've played around with my feelings, denying them any credibility, denying your own, so terrified of commitment, you couldn't even accept that you needed love just like anybody else—and now you can't even say goodbye without hiding behind role-playing exercises! What the hell is it with you? Why can't you just say what you feel?'

He stared at her, his mouth clamped into a grim line.

'Still nothing to say?' she goaded. 'Well, when you're ready to tell me—to my face, from your heart—what you feel, come and find me. Maybe I'll speak to you——'

She turned away, her voice cracking, and waited for the sound of his footsteps.

Nothing. Just an endless, breathless silence.

'Come back to the cottage,' he said eventually.

'No.'

'Please. I want to talk to you.'

'You, or a thirty-two-year-old professional man?' she asked sarcastically, hardly daring to hope. 'Are you sure there's anything to say?'

He hesitated. She heard him drag in a deep breath, then he spoke, very softly. 'There's a lot I want to say, Abbie. I just hope I haven't left it too late to say it.'

She turned, very slowly, unable to believe the sincerity she had heard in his voice.

'Please?'

She went, heart in her mouth, telling Tom on the way past to finish loading the car and wait for her.

Leo opened the car door for her in grim-lipped silence, the first time he had shown any gentlemanly urge to do so, and then went round and let himself in, gunning the engine and shooting out into the Saturday morning traffic.

She closed her eyes and hung on, and a few minutes later they turned into the drive of his cottage and skidded to a halt.

'Where's the fire?' she asked weakly.

He let out his breath on a harsh sigh. 'Sorry. I just wanted to get this over.'

He opened her door again, and then showed her in. Tiger purred and yowled round her ankles, and Leo scooped him up and shut him in the kitchen.

Then he turned to Abbie.

'Um—I don't know where to start.'

'Try opening your mouth and just talking,' she said shortly. Her heart was pounding, and she could hardly bear the suspense.

'You aren't going to make this any easier, are you?' he asked bitterly.

'No way. I'm not putting words in your mouth so you can turn round to me later and say I tricked you——'

'Is that what you really think I'd do?'

'I don't know what I think. As sure as eggs I don't know what you think, but if you don't tell me soon I shall walk home.'

His eyes fluttered closed, and when he opened them they were brighter than ever, the blue burning like flames, touched with pure gold.

'I love you,' he said at last. 'I didn't realise until I knew you were going. All this week I've been trying to come to terms with the funny feeling I had. It took me till last night, and then I realised what it was—pain. I was being torn in half, and a part of me was being taken away.'

He reached out his hands, and she took them, staring into his glittering blue eyes.

'Marry me, Abbie,' he said unevenly. 'Stay—finish your training. You can take all the hospice work—next year they're talking about being able to afford a part-time permanent doctor on the staff. You'd be ideal. You could work part-time in the practice——Hell, Abbie, talk to me!'

'Yes,' she said softly.

'Yes? Yes what?'

She laughed, the sound like music to his ears.

'Yes, I'll marry you. Yes, I'll finish my training—if I can do the hospice work. And yes, I'll take the job next year if they offer it to me. OK?'

He nodded dumbly.

'Leo?'

He was staring at her, looking slightly shell-shocked.

'Kiss me, please.'

He moved then, a great groan erupting from his body as he cupped her cheeks in his hands and lowered his mouth to hers, sealing their pledge.

Finally he lifted his head and wrapped his arms round her, crushing her against his chest. 'Oh, Abbie, I thought I'd lost you. . .'

She couldn't answer — not because she was speechless. There was a great deal she wanted to say, not least how much she loved him. But until he released her, just a little — still, it would keep. It felt too wonderful to be in his arms again, and the last thing she was going to do was complain, even if all her ribs were creaking.

'Are you OK?' he asked her a minute later.

She nodded, and his arms slackened.

'I love you,' she told him, and this time he didn't turn away from her. Instead he kissed her, very gently.

'I love you too, you aggravating little witch.'

'Good. It's time you were caught.'

He grinned. 'I thought it would feel claustrophobic, but it doesn't, does it?'

'No, it doesn't. It feels right.'

She leant away from him, staring up into his eyes. They really were the most amazing blue, she thought absently.

'Why were you so gun-shy?' she asked curiously.

'Gun-shy?'

'Mmm. Such a confirmed bachelor. I mean, my brother's a confirmed bachelor, but you're nothing like him. He would really hate to be settled, but you've got a house, and a garden that you love, and even a cat — '

He snorted. 'Yes, well, the less we say about that the better.'

She chuckled. 'So, anyway, you aren't real bachelor material, so why the great determination never to get married or saddle yourself with a family? You've mentioned it so many times — about the Clarkes, about the Tanners — what is it that frightens you?'

His eyes clouded and he drew her close again.

'Losing you,' he said quietly. 'Working in the hospice, I've seen so many times the havoc caused by grief. Look at the Tanners — torn apart by Mary's death. It came at just the wrong time with us, of course, just when I was beginning to feel the first stirrings of what could have been love.'

He sighed. 'I thought if I could pretend I didn't love you, then it wouldn't hurt when you went away.' He gave a short, hollow laugh. 'That was the theory. In practice, of course, as soon as I knew you were going, my heart started giving me hell.' He hugged her hard. 'I love you, Abbie. The thought of life without you was more than I could bear.'

'Oh, Leo — so all this nonsense was just a way of convincing yourself that you didn't need someone to love?'

'I suppose so,' he said quietly. 'It's worked up to now, but then I suppose that's because I hadn't met you. You're very special, Abbie.'

She hugged him, tears filling her eyes. 'Oh, Leo, you're very special too. I hope I never lose you, but if I do I'll be much richer for having known you.'

'Oh, God, Abbie. . .'

His mouth found hers, his lips gentle, his kiss a tender supplication.

After an age his lifted his head and cradled her close. 'Oh, my darling, to think I nearly lost you because I was too afraid to reach out and dare to love you.'

'You are silly,' she told him softly. 'And you'd better not change your mind, because I have no intention of letting you go now, not ever.'

'Good. It's mutual. You'd better ring your brother and tell him to bring all your stuff here — it'll be harder to run away if you're trapped with me in my lair.'

'Sounds exciting,' she murmured, her fingers busy with his shirt buttons. 'But I'll call him later, if you don't mind. I've got plans for you just now.'

He trapped her fingers. 'Later. I haven't finished telling you how much I love you.'

'So show me,' she challenged.

His eyes sparkled, and he reached for her. 'My pleasure. . .'

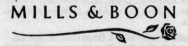

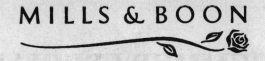

MILLS & BOON

LOVE ON CALL
4 FREE BOOKS AND 2 FREE GIFTS
FROM MILLS & BOON

Capture all the drama and emotion of a hectic medical world when you accept 4 Love on Call romances PLUS a cuddly teddy bear and a mystery gift - absolutely FREE and without obligation. And, if you choose, go on to enjoy 4 exciting Love on Call romances every month for only £1.80 each! Be sure to return the coupon below today to: Mills & Boon Reader Service, FREEPOST, PO Box 236, Croydon, Surrey CR9 9EL.

--- **NO STAMP REQUIRED** ---

YES! Please rush me 4 FREE Love on Call books and 2 FREE gifts! Please also reserve me a Reader Service subscription, which means I can look forward to receiving 4 brand new Love on Call books for only £7.20 every month, postage and packing FREE. If I choose not to subscribe, I shall write to you within 10 days and still keep my FREE books and gifts. I may cancel or suspend my subscription at any time. I am over 18 years. Please write in BLOCK CAPITALS.

Ms/Mrs/Miss/Mr _____ **EP63D**

Address _____

_____

Postcode _____ Signature _____

mps
MAILING
PREFERENCE
SERVICE